THEY'RE EVERY COLOR, SIZE, AND SHAPE. THEY'RE SCARED, THEY'RE BRAVE. THEY'RE RICH, THEY'RE POOR. THEY'VE GOT NOTHING IN COMMON BUT A DREAM THAT ONE DAY THE WHOLE WORLD WILL KNOW THEIR NAMES. A DREAM OF FAME.

DORIS—pushed and prodded by her stage mother, she had to learn to be beautiful on her own.

MONTGOMERY—he needed to come to terms with loneliness, and with his sexuality.

RALPH—his intensity and anger threatened to drive him to the same fate that claimed his idol, Freddie Prinze.

LEROY—an outlaw from Harlem, he found that his passion for dancing was transforming his life.

COCO—she thought she knew everything about being a performer, until life taught her some hard lessons.

IF THEY'VE REALLY GOT WHAT IT TAKES, IT'S GONNA TAKE EVERYTHING THEY'VE GOT.

METRO-GOLDWYN-MAYER

Presents

An ALAN PARKER Film

"FAME"

Written by CHRISTOPHER GORE

Produced by DAVID DE SILVA and
ALAN MARSHALL

Directed by ALAN PARKER

FAME

A Novel By
Leonore Fleischer

Based on the Alan Parker film

Screenplay by
Christopher Gore

FAWCETT GOLD MEDAL • NEW YORK

FAME

Published by Fawcett Gold Medal Books, a unit of CBS Publications, the Consumer Publishing Division of CBS Inc.

The author and publisher are grateful for permission to reprint the following:

Passage from THE DARK AT THE TOP OF THE STAIRS by William Inge is reprinted by permission of International Creative Management, 40 W. 57th Street, New York, N.Y. 10019 as agent for said play. Copyright 1945 as an unpublished work by William Inge under the title "Farther Off From Heaven." © Copyright 1958 by William Inge. © Copyright 1960 by William Inge (revised).

Excerpt from MARTY by Paddy Chayefsky is copyright © 1953 by Paddy Chayefsky. Reprinted courtesy of Paddy Chayefsky.

ISBN: 0-449-14359-7

Printed in the United States of America

First Fawcett Gold Medal printing: May 1980

10 9 8 7 6 5 4 3 2 1

For Helen, and it's about time, too

—L.G.F.

AUDITIONS

"DORIS? Doris! Wake up, baby. It's *today*. This is it, Doris. Our day."

Squeezing her eyelids tightly shut, Doris Finsecker pressed her face into her pillow. If only her mother's voice would go away! But it never did. It never, never went away, and it wouldn't now. Especially not today.

"Get up, Doris. I want you to have a good, nourishing hot breakfast before we go. We have to look our best and sound our best, baby. Today they're gonna be looking at us." Her mother was standing at the foot of Doris's bed, fully dressed, her hair out of its rollers. Ready for The Day.

A long shudder shook Doris's small frame as she tried to sit up. Breakfast. She couldn't stand even the sound of the word, not with the clenched knot of nervousness squeezing the breath out of her chest. She

9

fought down a wave of nausea. She felt limp, exhausted. She hadn't closed her eyes all night long, dreading the morning.

It didn't occur to Doris that, all over New York City, thirteen hundred boys and girls were waking up with exactly the same set of symptoms—cramps, nausea, shortness of breath and a feeling of doom. Today was The Day for them, too.

"You get dressed, Doris. I put out the dress you should wear. Put on your brown shoes with the straps; I polished them last night. I'll go poach the eggs."

Poached eggs, yechhh. Doris stood up, not daring to glance at the foot of the bed where her dress was laid out. Not the one with the little white top and the Peter Pan collar. She looked twelve years old in that dress. Please, not that one! She looked. It was the dress with the little white top and the Peter Pan collar. Sighing, Doris went to wash up. This was going to be the worst day of her entire life. I'll never get through it alive, she thought. I'll never even make it past the poached eggs.

Up in Harlem, about fifteen miles and one hundred and fifty light-years away from the Finsecker apartment in Brooklyn, Shirley Mullholland was tying red bows into her hair, peering anxiously into the cracked mirror. In the bed behind her, her little sister was still asleep. Accidentally, Shirley's fingers twisted too hard around the ribbon and painfully pulled a tuft of hair.

"Ow! Shit!" That Leroy, he better show up. She had told him and told him how important it was for him to be there, but Leroy, he just shrugged and smiled that little smile of his. He had practiced the routine with her, but it was only because he liked to dance. He was so independent, so cool, that today he just might take himself a walk. Today of all days. This was her only chance. If she didn't make it today, then maybe she never would. They looked at four thousand, but they chose only two hundred. Leroy, you better get here. And you better be ready to dance.

Montgomery MacNeill stared up at the ceiling of his large, nearly empty bedroom. One in twenty. They picked one in twenty. Funny, he hadn't thought he was going to be nervous, but he was. A tight knot of fear was pulsing under his ribs, somewhere below his diaphragm. They held three days of auditions, and about thirteen hundred kids were auditioned on each of the days. Of those four thousand, only two hundred got in. Only seventy of them were chosen for the drama department. So it was like seventy out of four thousand. What were the odds? He didn't want to think about them.

Why was he so nervous? After all, he was pretty well prepared. He knew his reading by heart. And he was at least one jump up on most of the people auditioning today. He'd had private professional training; he'd studied with a voice coach and an acting coach. And, if he didn't get in, what was the big deal? Performing Arts wasn't the only school in the world. He could go on to yet another private school. The knot tightened.

As Dr. Golden had taught him, Montgomery tried to analyze his feelings. Why did his guts twist at the thought of another private school? He didn't want to be sent away again. He hated the feeling of being set apart, the feeling that tutors and coaches and private schools gave him. The feeling of being *different*. For once in his life, he wanted to be like everybody else . . . at least, as far as he *could* be. He needed to mix with life for a change, meet it on everyday terms, see what it was *really* like out there. Locked inside his private world, he felt so cut off from reality sometimes, so lonely. He *needed* this school. He needed the High School of Performing Arts. He *had* to pass this audition. He *had* to.

Coco Hernandez wiggled to a disco beat as she threw her leotards into her dance bag. Today is *mine*, she told herself. I've been waiting for this day for months. I'll kill the people, they'll die when they see me. Little Miss Talent, you are on your way. Look out, Broadway. Hollywood, shake in your tap shoes. Ms. Coco is on her way. *If* you pass the audition. What the hell do you mean, if? she demanded, furious with herself. You mean *when*. Ain't no ifs about Coco Hernandez. Even a blind man can see I'm gonna be a *star*. Gonna shine, starting today. But, as she tugged on the zipper to close her overstuffed bag, her hands trembled, and the cold sweat on her palms made her fingers slip on the zipper-pull. The hell with it. Coco picked up the unzipped bag and slammed the door of her tenement apartment behind her.

In a seven-room house in the heart of Astoria, Queens, Bruno Martelli woke up with the smell of his mother's bitter black coffee in his nostrils. At first he just lay on his back, drowsy, wishing he could go back to sleep. Downstairs in the kitchen, he could hear his mother banging cups and saucers, and the rough male voices of his father and his uncle. His Uncle Mario? What was he doing here on a weekday morning? Then he remembered. It was today. He sat up in bed, and looked instinctively at the appointment postcard tucked into his dresser mirror. It was today, all right. The audition. Bruno groaned and dropped his head back onto the pillow. Now he really wanted to go back to sleep!

Playing in public for other people to approve or disapprove was not Bruno's bag. Why couldn't they leave him be, comfortable, safe and happy, downstairs in the basement? He'd fixed it up like a studio, and he spent countless hours down there, hunched over his keyboards, his huge earphones carrying his music directly to his ears and nobody else's. That was contentment to Bruno Martelli. That was all he asked out of life, not this competitive stuff. Competition wasn't for the truly creative.

But he had to go to high school, didn't he? And it had better be a high school where music was important, where his inner drives would be treated with respect. So it had to be Performing Arts. Which meant he had to pass the audition. Which meant he had to get up. Now.

I'm gonna get in. I *gotta* get in. On the subway all the way down from the south Bronx, Ralph told himself over and over, I'm gonna make it. I'm gonna get in. Folded tightly in his jeans pocket was the postcard with the appointment on it. Today. Please report at 9:30 A.M., read the card. Board of Education, City of New York, High School of Performing Arts, read the

13

card, with an address on West 46th Street in Manhattan. It was a good school, even a great school. Some dynamite performers had studied there—stars as varied as Liza Minnelli, Al Pacino, Melissa Manchester. Dom de Luise. And Freddie. Freddie Prinze. Only Freddie hadn't graduated, he'd been kicked out. A troublemaker. So cool, Freddie. Only a couple of years after they'd kicked him out, he'd come back in a Cadillac El Dorado, customized job, with a couple of blondes hanging around his neck. Came back to the old school and let them take a good look at him, admire him. Him, someday it would be him, Ralph Garcy. They'd all look up to Ralph Garcy as they looked up to Freddie. "But I gotta get into Freddie's old school. I gotta." Unconsciously, he'd spoken aloud, and he looked around himself in embarrassment. Hell, nobody even looked up. On the New York subways, you could come in the door riding an elephant and leading a parade, and nobody would look up. Nobody would care.

Someday he, Ralph Garcy, would make them care. They'd all look up when he came strutting by, and they'd all whisper his name, getting a thrill. He'd be famous. But first, he had to pass this goddamn audition. And he had no idea what he was even gonna do.

The seedy building housing the High School of Performing Arts was old when George Burns was a boy. It had been built in 1908 as a firehouse, and later passed from official hand to official hand, until it was allotted to the drama, dance and music departments of the school. The first graduating class in that building was 1948 (Eartha Kitt was in that one) and for the next thirty years the ancient stone structure echoed with the tuning up of instruments, the slap of feet in ballet slippers and the cries and groans issuing from drama rehearsals.

For twelve of those thirty years Al Farrell had endured the annual torment of auditions. As head of the drama department, it fell to his lot to watch and hear the recitals of a thousand or so hopefuls every year. For three long days in December, before the Christmas break, boys and girls from the five boroughs of New York trooped in, straggled in, tiptoed in, clutching the precious appointment postcard. They subjected Farrell to the anguish of hearing some of the finest words written in the English language mangled and tortured beyond recognition.

Few of these kids had any real talent. It was Farrell's job, along with the heads of the dance and music departments, to discover the few in which the true flame burned, to nurture that spark, until it could explode into flame. Given the fact that all the kids auditioning for P.A. were terrified and nervous, it was sometimes hard to discern that spark. Farrell felt the weight of the responsibility, and it was a heavy one. What if real talent should slip through his fingers, hidden under the nervous spasms of a poor audition? What if he were to turn away, to reject a girl who could grow up to be another Jane Fonda or Colleen Dewhurst? Or a boy who might have been a young Sidney Poitier? Talent was so rare, so precious—to

15

deny it was a grave sin in Farrell's own set of commandments.

So the ordeal of audition day was a mixture of anxiety, boredom and an occasional feeling of elation when a boy or girl, sometimes confidently but more often falteringly, showed a touch of that special inner something, that indefinable non-substance that is . . . talent. For the sake of those rare moments, dedicated teachers like Al Farrell existed.

He felt that elation now, as he sat in the fourth row of the tiny "theatre," listening to the boy sitting alone on the chair on the platform above, reciting his audition. This boy had it, talent. Farrell's eyes flicked over the boy's application on his clipboard.

MacNeill, Montgomery. He'd had previous acting training, some classes at the Academy, a coach. And wasn't he Marcia MacNeill's son? Yes, here it was, on the application next to "Mother's name." A very good actress, erratic, sometimes mannered, but an intelligent player who chose her vehicles thoughtfully. And beautiful. The boy looked nothing like her.

Farrell turned his attention to Montgomery again. He saw a thin, pale redheaded boy, tall for his age, his face and body exhibiting an adult kind of repose. The boy's narrow face bore deep-set dark-gray eyes, so heavy-lidded that they wore a look of patient sadness, a wide mouth, strong jaw lines. The face was crowned by a thick froth of curly red hair. An expressive face, it was one he was going to have to grow into. There was more of the man than the boy in it.

For his audition, Montgomery had selected a speech from William Inge's *The Dark at the Top of the Stairs*. It was, reflected Farrell, a refreshing change from Mark Antony's funeral oration from *Julius Caesar;* if he had heard "Friends, Romans, and countrymen," once today, he'd heard it two hundred times, and not once spoken with any understanding of the lines. The Inge passage was simple, yet it made a statement. A statement about pain, longing, loneliness and abandonment.

Pain, longing, loneliness, abandonment—these were feelings Montgomery MacNeill was too familiar with. He spoke the lines simply, without any attempt at instilling them with "feeling." The feeling was already there. He spoke softly, yet his light baritone projected off the dais and into the seats, where sat his "audience" of one.

" 'I always worry that maybe people aren't going to like me when I go to a party. Isn't that crazy? Do you ever get kind of a sick feeling in the pit of your stomach when you dread things? Gee, I wouldn't want to miss a party for anything. But every time I go to one . . . I keep feeling that the whole world's against me. See,' " and here the boy let his eyes drop to his folded hands, " 'see, I've spent my whole life in military academies. My mother doesn't have a place for me where she lives. She . . . she just doesn't know what else to do with me. But you mustn't misunderstand about my mother. She's really a very lovely person.' "

In the darkened seats below, Farrell permitted himself a slight smile. The boy seemed to be telling him the story of his own life.

" 'I guess every boy thinks his mother is beautiful, but my mother really is,' " continued Montgomery wistfully. " 'She tells me in every letter she writes how sorry she is that we can't be together more, but she has to think of her work. One time we were together, though. She met me in San Francisco once and we were together for two whole days.' "

Montgomery lifted his head and his lips curved in a slight smile at the happy remembrance. Farrell found himself smiling back. " 'Just like we were sweethearts. It was the most wonderful time I ever had. And then I had to go back to the military academy. Every time I walk into the barracks, I get kind of . . . kind of . . .' " Montgomery broke off, his voice choking, not with emotion but with panic. He had forgotten the line. Quickly, almost frantically, he scanned the paper in his lap, finding the line with some difficulty. "Sorry," mumbled the boy. He'd muffed it. I've screwed it up, he told himself, humiliated. Damn. Finding the line, he continued the speech.

" '. . . kind of a depressed feeling. It's got hard stone walls . . . you know what I mean. Well, gee! I guess I've bored you enough, telling you about myself.' " Montgomery finished and waited silently, his deep-set eyes probing for a reaction from Mr. Farrell.

"Thank you," said Farrell quietly. He was a handsome, balding black man in a crew-neck sweater and dungarees.

"Sorry about that," Montgomery said in a stifled voice. "I goofed the last couple of lines. Nervous, I guess." I'll never make it, he thought. I'll never get in now.

"That's okay." Farrell smiled briefly. "You did very well." He's in, he thought, making a large check mark on the application form on his clipboard. He's very talented. And for some reason, very, very sad. Throughout the next two bumbling, horrible auditions, Farrell kept remembering Montgomery MacNeill's brooding, sensitive face.

════════════════════

It's going to be a very long day, thought Vladimir Shorofsky with a barely muffled moan. As head of Performing Arts' music department, he had already heard a hundred and fifty would-be musicians mangling Mozart and pummeling Puccini. So far today, he had selected about thirty youngsters who appeared to know which end of the instrument made the music. Of the thirty, perhaps five possessed genuine musical talent. Thirty out of a hundred and fifty. What a waste of time, money and effort the other hundred and twenty represented! Mostly, it was the parents' fault, thought Shorofsky, shaking his heavy gray head and pushing his eyeglasses back up his sizable nose. Because *they* couldn't read a note of music, they insisted that their children become prodigies. What a waste! He nodded to the young Korean boy whose turn had come. The boy flicked his heavy black hair out of his eyes with a sharp turn of the head. Cradling his violin lovingly under his chin, the boy launched into a piece by Bartók.

The strains of music rose from the violin in swells of elegant melody, as precise as a sword's edge, as dainty as a deer's hooves. Unconsciously, Shorofsky smiled broadly with pleasure, as his sharp ears assessed the boy's technique. There was promise here, real promise. Perhaps one day he would be a solo artist. He still needed work, but what else are we here

19

for? As the short selection ended, and the boy lowered his bow, Shorofsky nodded vigorously.

"Thank you. You play very well."

The Korean boy nodded back gravely.

"Now, Mrs. Tossoff will play some notes, and you will sing them back to me." He turned to his assistant, a plump woman in her middle fifties who sat poised at the piano in the large music room.

"Like this." Mrs. Tossoff played the scales, once up and once down. Shorofsky echoed them, his "la las" booming from his heavy chest. "You understand?" he demanded of the boy, who was looking a little dubious.

"La la la LA la la la," went the piano.

"La la la LA la la la," went the boy, very softly. Almost no sound came from his shy lips.

"Louder!" barked Mr. Shorofsky, chewing at his moustache. "Sing louder! I'm testing your ears, not your voice!" My God, he thought, it's going to be a very, very long day.

The dance department was in its usual state of audition-time bedlam. The long, high-ceilinged room echoed with the hard slap of toe shoes, the insistent rhythms of the accompanying piano and the chattering voices of close to a hundred girls.

Girls, thought Miss Evelyn Berg for the two hundredth time. I get nothing but girls. Don't boys ever want to dance? Here and there in the throng was an isolated boy, only a handful of them all together, and most of them looking ill-at-ease. The girls, on the other hand, were chirping away like a collection of starlings. From time to time, as if to emphasize the re-

20

semblance, they would flutter their wings, shake their feathers, and prepare to fly. Over against the mirrored wall, half a dozen girls were working out at the barre, supervised by a teacher in a leotard. Miss Berg and two student monitors sat at the far end of the room, at a long table covered by a scattered mess of application forms and empty coffee containers. The table commanded an excellent view of the floor. As the latest group of auditioning dancers, twenty girls and one boy, swept past her in a series of classical steps, Miss Berg's heavy dark brows drew together over her large, expressive eyes. *What makes these children so determined to dance? How many of them have any idea of the difficulties of a dancer's way of life? They starve themselves down*—at least, most of them do—(and here she frowned at a couple of hefty youngsters jammed into tight leotards) *and they grow their hair long, and they think they're Makarova or Judith Jamison. Klutzes. That's what we've got here. Mostly klutzes.* Frowning, Miss Berg shook her dark head from side to side. *This bunch was hopeless. Where was the next group? Why weren't they ready?*

"Attention, please!" she called out, as a student monitor pushed the next group out onto the polished floor. "Please!" Miss Berg waited for silence, which eventually arrived. "Thank you. The first thing I want you to do is just walk across the floor, so we can get a good look at you and see what your bodies are like."

Lisa Monroe groaned, looked around unhappily and took a few steps backward so that she would be partly hidden in the second row, where she hoped the head of the dance department couldn't see her body too well. She *hated* her body, which was a little on the

21

soft side for a dancer. Most of the girls around her, black or white, shared the thin intensity of Miss Berg. They *looked* like dancers. Well, I've got five tutus, she consoled herself. Maybe I should have worn one of them instead of these dancer's tights. But then she'd be one of only two or three girls in the vast room wearing a ballet skirt. And she didn't want to stand out. Not today. I want to pass, but not to stand out. Lisa turned to the girl on her left, an angular black girl with an air of great hauteur, like an Egyptian queen. The girl's hair was dressed in long, tight braids, about a dozen of them, and she had pierced her nose and placed a hoop of gold in the nostril.

"I like your ring," said Lisa timidly. "Does it hurt or is it ethnic?"

The Egyptian queen turned her head in great disdain away from Lisa. Angrily, she hissed at the girl on the other side of her, "I'm not singing."

"You have to," the girl whispered back loudly.

"I came here to dance," insisted the girl in the nose ring. Her name was Phenicia.

"You have to sing, too," insisted the shorter girl stubbornly. "And act. And play a musical instrument."

Phenicia gave her a bitter smile of disbelieving, royal scorn. "Oh, sure."

"It says Performing *Arts,* doesn't it?" the other girl demanded, stressing the plural.

"You don't have to do everything," Phenicia said.

"It helps, baby," put in Coco Hernandez, from the front row. She spoke out of the side of her mouth, so Miss Berg wouldn't spot her. "It sure as shit helps." Me, I do everything.

22

The music was striking up now, and unconsciously the girls—and the single boy—stood straighter, stretching their necks to make them look swanlike, and their waists to give their bodies length and grace.

"After that, we'll give you a number and two minutes apiece to see what you've prepared," called Miss Berg. She stood up and came around the table so that she could see the dancers better. She was a tall woman in her mid-thirties, with sharp collarbones and long hair caught up in a dancer's bun.

"I hate my legs," Lisa confided to the girl on the other side of her.

"All right now," Miss Berg called out. "One by one. In time to the music."

"I tried every diet in the world when I was young," continued Lisa, although the girl she was speaking to showed no signs of listening. "But you can't help your genes. Jeez, I'm so nervous. I like your scarf."

The piano settled into a slow march, and one at a time the girls slowly crossed the room, holding their heads high, under the critical gaze of Miss Berg.

She watched them impatiently. Only one or two of them seemed to have the makings of a dancer. Maybe three at most. Under her breath, she asked herself for the two hundred and first time that day, "Where are the boys?"

Mrs. Sherwood sat like a rock of calm in an ocean of noise. Although she dreaded audition days, with their noisy influx of panic-stricken teenagers who didn't know where anything was or where they were supposed to be or what forms they were supposed to have with them, she managed to preserve a cool exterior. These kids needed help and, as an academic teacher, Barbara Sherwood was mercifully not involved in judging their talent, only in seeing to it that they went up the right staircase in the right order, carrying the right papers. She guarded her desk as if it was a command post. In fact, it was—a combination of information center and security blockhouse, and it stood directly in front of the staircase leading to the audition rooms. You had to pass Mrs. Sherwood before you could get upstairs.

"Name?" she demanded, of a chunky black girl and a slim black boy.

"Er . . . excuse me, miss, you don't need his name he's not here for an audition he's my partner see . . ." the girl answered loudly and quickly over her thick wad of chewing gum.

"What school is he from?" asked Mrs. Sherwood, looking the boy over. He was tall and good-looking, with bright brown skin and large eyes that tilted upward at the corners. The corners of his mouth turned up in an insolent smile to match his arrogant eyes. He stared back at the white teacher.

Shirley shrugged and her words tumbled out, louder and quicker than before. "He ain't into school he's just helpin' me out see with my dancin' . . . he's just a partner we've been rehearsin' together but it's me who's auditioning . . . Mullholland see Shirley and I'm all fixed up I filled in all your forms and all . . ." The chunky girl waved a handful of forms.

Mrs. Sherwood shook her head calmly. She was in

24

no hurry. "He doesn't go upstairs without filling in his name."

"Leroy's his name." The girl slowed down a little. "But it's me who's auditioning. Shirley Mullholland. Two l's." She leaned over the desk and whispered loudly, "And don't ask him to do no writing, miss. He gets real mean at that."

The intimation of a smile appeared behind Mrs. Sherwood's eyes. "Doesn't he talk?"

Shirley shrugged again. "He ain't into conversation, miss. Not until you know him."

With a raised eyebrow, Mrs. Sherwood wrote down "Leroy," then looked up at the boy again. He was staring calmly over her head, as though interested in something behind her. But the expression on his face—cool, remote, insolent—hadn't changed.

"Leroy what?" the teacher asked.

"Johnson. Leroy Johnson. Now can we go up?"

"If he's going up, he'll have to check his knife," replied Mrs. Sherwood matter-of-factly. Without leaning over, she picked up a ruler and used it to raise Leroy's sweatshirt, revealing a large hunting knife in a leather sheath at the boy's waist. Leroy didn't move; his eyes barely flicked down.

"He ain't stayin' long enough for trouble, miss," insisted Shirley nervously. "He's just helpin' out a friend."

Mrs. Sherwood's voice was pleasant and informative. "He's not helping out anyone unless he checks his knife. This is the High School of Performing Arts. We don't cut one another up here. We leave that to the critics."

Leroy pursed his lips and, with a single careless

25

movement, whipped the knife out of its sheath. He held it out to Mrs. Sherwood, a few inches beyond her reach. "You want it?" he said, and he grinned.

"I want it." Mrs. Sherwood made no move to take it. For a long moment the woman and the boy stared silently at each other, as if each was taking the other's measure. Then Leroy's smile broke out again, as fresh as the paint on the henhouse door. "You promise you won't steal it?" he asked her arrogantly, flipping the knife onto her desk.

Mrs. Sherwood didn't bother to reply. She simply jerked her head at the stairs, giving Shirley and Leroy silent permission to pass.

"Thanks, sugar." The grateful Shirley was sweating profusely from sheer nervousness as she led the way up the noisy staircase.

Leroy shrugged. "I got lotsa knives," he told her nonchalantly, opening his jacket. The lining was hung with knives, eight or ten of them.

Shirley gave a little gasp of dismay. That Leroy!

"We know our rights. You can't refuse her an audition."

The strident tones of Mrs. Finsecker's voice caused Mr. Farrell to wince and shake his head.

"She's not supposed to sing her audition. You were told that. This is a drama department," he said again, with all the patience he could call upon. He looked up at the ministage, feeling sorry for the fourteen-year-old girl who stood there nervously, her eyes on the floor, her hands twisting the skirt of her childish dress.

Doris Finsecker kept her eyes down, wishing hopelessly that her ordeal were over, and she could leave this terrifying place. And yet, something had drawn her to it, a kind of vitality, an excitement that she felt as soon as she turned down West 46th Street and saw the ancient stone building that was her first glimpse of Performing Arts.

Doris had always attended cement-block-and-glass schools in the neat middle-class neighborhood where she'd grown up. This was so different! When they'd come out of the subway into Times Square, Mrs. Finsecker had grasped Doris's hand firmly in hers and had practically dragged her through the sweaty mass of derelict humanity thronging the streets. Doris had stared fascinated at the three-card monte games, the young men openly selling drugs, the tall black men dressed in white robes, hawking the Black Muslim newspaper, the lightly dressed hookers in their high boots and miniskirts, wrapped tightly in patchwork rabbit-fur jackets against the crisp December weather. There was so much life here, and it fascinated Doris. Her excitement grew as she approached the school and watched dozens of boys and girls trooping through the doors, laughing and calling remarks to one another. They seemed so free, so independent.

Once inside, Doris had seen almost instantly that what she had feared was true: there weren't any other mothers present at the auditions. Well, maybe one or two, but almost all the kids had come alone. Doris felt like a baby, stupid and not to be trusted out by herself. Weeks ago, she had timidly broached the subject of going by herself. Mrs. Finsecker had made such short work of it that Doris knew better than to raise it again. Now she stood on the tiny stage in the drama department, listening in humiliation while her mother pushed in where she didn't belong. She could hear the black teacher saying, "This is a drama department," and her mother's reply.

"When she sings, it *is* drama."

Doris shuddered, but she didn't raise her eyes or open her mouth. She was aware of four people below her—her mother, Mr. Farrell the teacher, and two student monitors who were helping him with the auditions. One of them was a tall, extremely good-looking boy with bright blue eyes and carefully styled hair.

"What's your name?" Doris heard the teacher call out gently to her, but before she could answer, her mother yelled, "Finsecker."

"Doris Finsecker," said Doris without looking up.

Mrs. Finsecker had stationed herself just outside the auditorium door, where she could see and hear everything, but as Mr. Farrell addressed her daughter she abandoned even this pretense and openly came into the room, taking a seat at the rear.

"Who taught you?" asked Mr. Farrell.

Doris opened her mouth to speak, but Mrs. Finsecker got there first.

"Barbra Streisand," she told him. "She has all her records. She saw *A Star Is Born* fourteen times. And I help her out."

"How's that?" Farrell addressed the question to Doris, who managed to get a word in. "Mama pays for my singing lessons. And sends me on commercial auditions," she said very quietly.

"I can't hear you," called Farrell.

"I'm sorry," murmured Doris, her face reddening. "What?"

"She's sorry," yelled Mrs. Finsecker, standing and almost trotting to the row where Farrell was sitting. Squeezing past the student monitors, she plunked herself down next to the teacher and confided, "She's a little nervous."

Farrell repressed a sigh. No matter how many times you heard the clichés about stage mothers, they all turned out to be true. He had seen this phenomenon about a dozen times in the years he'd been teaching here, and it never failed to pain him. Some shy kid, likely as not without an ounce of talent, being pressed and pushed and squeezed and twisted by the thwarted ambitions and doting misjudgment of an ambitious mother or father. He felt so sorry for these kids that he always gave them an extra measure of his strength and patience, although it never did any good. Those kids were hopeless, more like programmed robots or performing seals than genuinely talented actors or singers. Still, there was something very touching about this pale, shy girl standing humiliated on the stage. She had not yet become mechanical; her responses were not automatic, and she had completely forgotten to smile. Farrell was sure that Mrs. Finsecker had reminded her a thousand times to keep smiling no matter what.

"But she's not nervous when she sings," said Mrs. Finsecker in a wheedling voice.

"Why do you want to go to school here?" Mr. Farrell asked the girl gently.

To become part of all this energy, to become freer, thought Doris. But I can't say that, I can't tell him

29

that. "To . . . to . . . be in movies . . . or to be an actress," she stammered instead, telling Mr. Farrell what Mrs. Finsecker wanted to hear. She looked at her mother for her approval.

"What?" asked Farrell, cupping his ear.

Doris spoke up a little. "We can't afford a professional children's school," she said.

"Speak up, Doris," encouraged her mother.

Farrell sighed. May as well get this over with, and let the poor kid go. "Okay, if you want to sing, go ahead. Then we'll take a look at your acting."

"I'm a little nervous," said Doris, her lips trembling.

"Look at Michael," suggested Mr. Farrell. He pointed to the handsome blue-eyed boy at the end of the row. "Just sing to Michael. Don't worry about anyone else." It was an old entertainer's trick, and it almost always worked.

Doris looked at the boy, and her stomach did a tiny flip-flop. He was the best-looking boy she'd ever seen, and his blue eyes were looking right back at her. And he was smiling. It made her feel funny.

"I don't think I can do that," she said, dropping her eyes again and shaking her head. "I can't just stare."

"Think of it as a concentration exercise, all right?" As Doris hesitated, Farrell added, "He won't mind."

Michael nodded and his smile broadened as Doris stole another look at him. Uncertainly, she smiled back, then she nodded.

Immediately, Mrs. Finsecker put a small cassette player on the stage and punched the play button. A hesitant piano stumbled into "The Way We Were," with many wrong notes.

"That's her brother Harvey," whispered Mrs. Finsecker proudly. "He's nine and a half."

He plays like eight, thought Farrell with a wince.

Doris was singing now, her eyes fixed on Michael, who kept smiling, the grin splitting his face until it hurt.

. . Her voice was clear and could carry a tune, but it was thin and pitched too high for the song. Farrell felt an odd pang of disappointment as he listened to her. He had wanted her to be good. He had wanted to accept her, to work with her, to teach her confidence in herself and in her art. But she had no art.

Grinning happily, Mrs. Finsecker snapped an Instamatic picture of Doris as she sang. The explosion of the flashbulb caught Doris by surprise and made her hesitate in the song, but she picked it up after a moment's faltering, and her mother sank back down into her seat, beaming, an ecstatic tear stealing down her maternal cheek.

But now Doris had abandoned the music and was speaking the words. Her eyes remained locked on Michael's as she recited the story of loneliness and lost love, of words spoken and never forgotten, embraces once full and now empty.

Farrell sat up straighter, watching the slender girl on the stage take on life and color as she delivered the words of the popular song with conviction and a sensitive understanding that was instinctual, not learned. She seemed taller now, and her pale face with its large dark eyes shone from within. There was something there, after all. This was her own pain the girl was acting out on that stage; she must be really hurting. There were some interesting possibilities here, if she could only extract them and make them work for her. And if she could get out from underneath that mother of hers. He glanced at Mrs. Finsecker, who was weeping openly now as Doris picked up the music again for a strong finish. When the last notes died away, Mrs. Finsecker broke into noisy applause, causing Doris to blush furiously and drop her eyes again.

"That was very nice," said Farrell quietly. "Thank you. Oh, Doris," he began as though it were an afterthought. Doris looked up, her soft eyes meeting his. "What would you do if you don't make it?"

Doris hesitated, biting her lip.

"We'll make it," her mother stated grimly.

Mr. Shorofsky had to call "Next" three times, the last time a roar, before the thin Hispanic boy in the large, floppy overcoat put down his comic book and pointed innocently to his bony chest.

"Yes, you. What's your name?"

"Ralph Garcy."

"Who taught you?"

"My father," said Ralph promptly. It was hardly what the music teacher had expected to hear, and he said nothing. Ralph threw himself into the distrustful silence, thirty words a second. "He's doing work for the government now. I'm not supposed to talk about him. But he was very famous. He played in symphonies all over the world. Uh, he used to."

"What did he play?" Shorofsky asked dryly.

"Er . . ." Ralph tried to think of a symphony instrument. "Trombones." Shorofsky didn't nod. "And horns. French horns." More silence. Ralph was desperate to make an impression. "And English horns. And saxophones." He stopped and looked at the music teacher hopefully.

"Anything else?" asked Shorofsky sarcastically.

"Bongos and maracas," added Ralph, on safer ground.

"What did he teach you?" sighed Mr. Shorofsky, expecting the worst.

Reaching deep into his pocket, Ralph pulled out a small dime-store harmonica and waved it proudly. He put it to his lips and out came a cacophonous caterwauling that made Shorofsky squeeze his eyes shut in pain. He raised a hand to stop the boy, but that took a little doing now that Ralph was on a roll. Finally, with one last off-key wail, the harmonica mercifully ceased.

"Do you like to dance?" asked Mr. Shorofsky, his ears still aching.

"*Love* to dance," said Ralph with a grin.

"Then why don't you try the dance department?" suggested the music teacher, mopping at his forehead with an old handkerchief.

Farrell could not believe his ears. In the dozen or so years he'd spent at this school he had heard literally thousands of auditions, but nothing, *nothing* like this one. Of those thousands of readings, many hundreds had murdered Shakespeare, but this boy, having killed the Bard with his first line, was now jumping up and down on Shakespeare's mangled corpse.

"Uhhh . . . 'Romeo, Romeo, weerfaw are dow Romeo. Deny dy fadda and refuse dy name, or if dow wilt not, be but swawn my love,' " read the boy, his fingers underlining the words in the battered paperback, " 'and I'll no longer be a Cap . . . Cap . . . u . . .' "

" 'Capulet,' " offered Farrell, manfully trying not to break into hysterical laughter. This dumb kid was reading Juliet!

" 'Capulet,' " the boy went on doggedly. " ' 'Tis but dy name that is my enemy . . . Dow are dyself, dough not a Monta . . . Monta gyooooeee.' "

"Okay, hold it there," called Farrell. He doubted if he could keep it together another second. He was sure that the ghost of Will Shakespeare, thirsting for blood, would appear at any moment in the auditorium. "Look, this is the last day of auditions. We've seen a lot of students. It's late and we're a little punchy. I don't want to penalize you. Why don't you go next door and let Mrs. Shine audition you?" That ought to hand her a laugh, he thought.

"Uhhhh, sure ting." The boy picked up his jacket.

Farrell couldn't resist. "Oh, and by the way, you've been reading the girl's part," he said as casually as he could.

The boy on the stage executed a perfect double take. His mouth dropped open and he grabbed the book for a closer look. It was true. "Shhheeeesh!" .

When the auditorium door slammed angrily behind Juliet, Farrell doubled over clutching at his belly. The

34

laughter, so long repressed, rolled out of him in noisy, gasping waves. Now he'd heard everything!

━━━━━━━━━

Bruno Martelli turned around anxiously as he reached the school steps and watched his father and his Uncle Mario tussling with the huge synthesizer. They had pushed, pulled and wrestled it out of Angelo Martelli's cab, and were now carrying the heavy Arp AXXE up the sidewalk toward the Performing Arts building.

"Take it easy!" barked Angelo. "That's seven thousand worth of machine!"

"Dollars or pounds?" grunted Uncle Mario, trying not to let his end slip.

"Don't touch the rotary pots," Bruno called out.

"What pots?" asked Mario, confused. Nothing on the box but dials and switches and meters. What pots? Where pots?

"Or the V.C.O.," added Bruno. "I got it set on sawtooth." He was a tall boy with a thick head of curly black hair, and a dimpled face like a cherub in a painting of the Italian Renaissance. Under thick black brows, his eyes were a surprising blue, and they wore a serious, abstracted expression, now slightly worried as well. His arms were loaded with headphones, wires, yards and yards of coiled and snaky cable. A pair of speakers dangled from his overloaded fingers.

"Somebody get the door, please?" he asked the kids who were watching this procession of electronic gear make its way to the school. A sophomore girl pushed

35

the door open and held it while Bruno, followed by Angelo and Mario, struggled through. Once they had all this stuff in place, they had to go back to the cab for the keyboards.

Uncle Mario groaned as he felt the weight of the synthesizer getting to his weak back. "Why can't he play the piccolo or something sensible, or the accordion like Pappa did?" he complained to his brother.

Bruno's father shook his head. "Same reason you drive a Checker cab and not a Roman chariot, right? It's *progress*. My son's head is in the future. Besides, Pappa never could play the accordion." They wrestled the synthesizer inside the building and set it down, sweating.

"Music department, fifth floor," said a school monitor. "Take that staircase."

Uncle Mario groaned.

Although every nerve ending in her body told Miss Berg that this skinny Hispanic boy with the too-bright eyes and nervous manner was wrong for the dance department, she still listened as Ralph Garcy ran through his phony patter. After all, he was a boy, and she had been able to find only forty other suitable boys in three days of auditions. She nodded as though she believed Ralph.

"My father taught me. I'm not supposed to talk about him. He's doing work for the government now.

36

But he was famous. World-famous. He uh . . . he danced with the Rockettes." It was the only dance group Ralph had ever heard of.

Miss Berg closed her eyes in a moment of exquisite pain.

"Begin, please," she said quietly.

Ralph peeled off the comical overcoat that flapped, three sizes too big, around his 115-pound body. He was wearing a white cotton undershirt that clung to his bony chest and a tightly belted pair of pleated peg pants. On his feet were his "dancing shoes," a pair of high-topped basketball Keds fitted out with taps. "Do you know 'Swanee River'?" he asked the young woman at the piano.

The accompanist frowned, but nodded.

"Hit it."

The piano tinkled the old song, and Ralph began to dance. Clumsy, awkward, rhythmless, he jerked and tapped, executing the simplest time-steps so badly that Miss Berg could hardly believe her eyes. She had a parakeet at home who hopped around his cage more gracefully than this boy! He was hopeless, hopeless.

"Thank you," she called, to cut Ralph short.

Reluctantly, Ralph Garcy ground to a wobbly halt. "Pretty good, hah?" he demanded with a cocky grin.

It wasn't worth it. It just wasn't worth answering. Words could not begin to express how bad he was. "Why don't you try the drama department?" suggested Miss Berg. Anywhere but here.

Mr. Farrell slumped in his seat. He glanced at his clipboard; thank God the day was nearly over. Seven applications still remained; seven auditions to be heard. With any luck he could be out of here in an hour, on his way home to a hot shower and a kiss from his wife. All he had to do was to get through seven more; after all, how many surprises could they hold? If they didn't yield up another Montgomery MacNeill, surely they wouldn't be concealing another male Juliet.

"Sheila Robinson," he called.

Instantly, a tall black girl took the stage. She was large, massive, enormous. Maybe 240 pounds of flesh squeezed into a tight red T-shirt and a bulging pair of cutoff jeans. Mr. Farrell checked the impulse to laugh. He was worn out, but if he held it together only a little longer . . .

"I'm doin' *The Towering Inferno*. You know, the movie?"

Farrell nodded wearily. For a moment he considered stopping her, but curiosity got the better of him. "Go on," he said.

The big girl nodded back impassively. "I'm O. J. Simpson, see? Now I'm in this building. Now I'm walkin' to this elevator, see?" She took two short steps. Her mammoth breasts jiggled mightily, but the expression on her face didn't change one iota. "Now I push the button." One large brown hand came up slowly and pushed an imaginary button. "I'm waitin' for the elevator, see?" She waited. They all waited. A very long minute passed as they all waited for an elevator that didn't come. "Now I'm gettin' mad," declared Sheila Robinson without moving a facial or a body muscle. She didn't look mad; she didn't act mad. "Now I push the button again . . ."

Al Farrell opened his mouth to thank her and dismiss her, when a sudden flash overtook him, a burst of intuition that stunned him with its brilliance. This impassive fat girl, so calm, so almost somnolent on the stage, was the very stuff of which comedy was made. Her projection—unmovable sanity in a mad burning skyscraper—if taken, channeled, trained, could turn her into a great comic actor. She seemed perfectly at home on the stage; she had no nervous tics or twitches; in fact, he doubted if she could change her expression even if she wanted to. More than that, a sublimely funny air of perfect confidence surrounded her. She could be a female Buster Keaton. What a challenge! Decisively, Farrell put a large red check mark on her application. One more acceptance, and only six more auditions to get through.

Not yet discouraged, Ralph Garcy pulled the Pro Keds off his feet and tossed them into his bag. He barely glanced at the small thin girl sitting beside him on the floor, massaging her feet. So he was surprised when she spoke to him.

"Nobody talks about it, but there's a quota system. Your chances are better if you're black, or Puerto Rican . . . or everything. Like me."

Now Ralph looked at her. She was everything, all right. One of those tiny-boned Spanish black girls, as light and as nervous as a bird about to fly away. Her long hair was styled in a peculiar mix of tightly bound braids and loosely flowing locks. Her eyes were huge, as dark as lakes, with twin points of light dancing in them. Pretty as she was, she didn't appeal to Ralph. But she had challenged him.

"I *am* Puerto Rican."

"Not on paper, you're not," scoffed Coco Hernandez. " 'Ralph Garcy.' " Her voice put the phony name in quotes. "And all that noise about your daddy doin' work for the government . . ."

"That's the truth!" Ralph lied hotly.

But Coco had dug into his bag and pulled out his "dancing shoes," the basketball sneakers.

"Sure it is. And he left you his tap shoes, right?"

"Right," snapped Ralph.

"Does he work for Pepsi-Cola, too?" sneered Coco, turning the sneakers sole-side up. On the bottom Ralph had glued Pepsi-Cola bottle caps instead of taps.

Angry, humiliated, Ralph snatched the sneakers from Coco's grasp, stuffed them into his bag and stalked off without a word. Bitch! He had to find the drama department, and this time he'd have to do a lot better. It was his last chance to make it.

Shirley Mullholland had yet to dance a step, but she was already pretty uncomfortable. Maybe it had been a mistake to bring Leroy. Maybe she should have rehearsed a solo number. Here she was counting on him to be her partner, her *silent* partner, and

Leroy seemed to have lost all interest in the dance. Ever since they'd entered the dance room, Leroy had paid almost no attention to her. Those big eyes of his were tomcattin' around the room, checkin' out the chicks. And there were dozens and dozens of beautiful, slim black girls there, just waitin' for Leroy to check 'em out. Even the girl who had assigned them their number—80—had whispered something to Leroy that had made him grin and give her that "catch you later" look of his. Oh, yeah, he was handsome enough, with his broad-shouldered supple body, smooth brown skin and perfect teeth. But what the hell, wasn't he supposed to be *her* boyfriend? Sure didn't act like it. He was actin' like the heavens had opened and it was raining down ladies. That was the trouble with Leroy . . . you could never pin him down to *nothin.'* He always had a way of getting away from you, with a grin and a shrug of his shoulders . . .

"Number eighty," called Lydia, the senior student monitor who sat next to Miss Berg behind the long table.

"That's us!" Panic gripped Shirley, and she practically galloped out onto the dance floor. Leroy sauntered after her, cool. It was no skin off *his* behind; he wasn't studying going to no school.

Shirley put the cassette player down, and hit the music. The voice of Linda Clifford singing "Red Light" came pouring through the large speakers, and the couple started to dance.

After the first minute or two, Leroy started to get into it. At first, it took him by surprise to discover that they were the only couple on the floor, and that more than a hundred others, mostly girls, were watching him. He was accustomed to dancing in discos, where it was dark, noisy and crowded, and where everybody else was so busy doing his own thing he didn't have time to worry about yours. But, as the surprise wore off, he discovered that he liked it. He liked being out there on that floor, movin' so free and so fine, and having all those foxy ladies diggin' on his moves. He got into it, and began to get down. He pulled away from Shirley and let the music take him up solo. He had some funky moves to lay on these chicks.

Miss Berg's eyes widened as she watched the unmistakably sexual wrigglings and prancings of the tall boy on the floor. He had an innate grace that was startling, and he and the music appeared to be one.

"The girl's a disaster," she remarked to Lydia as they watched poor Shirley trying without hope of success to keep up with Leroy. Miss Berg pawed through the papers in front of her. "Where's his application form?" she demanded.

"He doesn't have one. He's here with her," said Lydia, not taking her eyes off Leroy, who was shaking his hips in a manner guaranteed to send lovin' ladies crazy.

"Get him an application," ordered Miss Berg.

"He's a mistake," protested Lydia.

"He's a boy and he dances. Get him an application!"

The music rose to fever pitch, hot, hotter, hottest. Leroy was shaking and grinding in place, his thighs swinging wildly, both feet planted without moving on the dance floor, letting his body talk. He felt cool and together, higher than he'd ever been. He could sense the admiration coming his way and, combined with his joy in movement, it gave him the best rush he'd ever experienced. He could dance here forever. He began making up new steps, inventing moves he'd never done before. Defeated and miserable, aware that the entire room was focused on Leroy and only on Leroy, Shirley stopped dancing and moved to one side. She glowered in anger and pain at Leroy but he was unaware of it. He was unaware of anything except the music and the power of his body. Dancing, he felt as powerful, as masterful and as aggressively masculine as the lion on the savannah. He placed one hand on his crotch and rubbed it suggestively, calling for his lioness. One hundred girls quivered.

"What do you call that?" breathed Miss Berg, her eyes glued to Leroy.

Completely turned on, Lydia giggled. "Wicked," she said.

"What's your name?" asked Mr. Farrell.

"Ralph Garcy. Uh—Raul Garcia."

"Who taught you?" It was the final audition of the day, thank God. This wiry, intense Hispanic boy was the last of them.

"My father. He's in Spain right now making Italian Westerns."

Uh-huh, thought Farrell. Out loud, he asked, "Why do you want to go to school here?"

The boy's expressive face went reverent. "Freddie went here."

"Freddie?" But Mr. Farrell knew.

"Freddie Prinze. He was the best."

"You want to be an actor." It was not a question, but a statement.

"Oh, sure." The skinny boy grinned nervously. "Judy, Judy, Judy," he parroted, a terrible imitation of Cary Grant. He squared his shoulders in the age-old Jimmy Cagney impression. "Top o' the world, Ma," he croaked.

I want to go home, thought Farrell. Right now. And because he felt that way—exhausted, bored, irritated—he had to go out of his way to be fair. To give this untalented, undirected kid the same amount of attention and care he'd given to serious youngsters like Montgomery MacNeill.

"We don't want you to perform," he told Garcia. "We want to see who *you* are. Do you understand?"

"Sure," said Ralph easily. He had no idea what the teacher was talking about.

"Use your own experience," Farrell instructed him earnestly. "Be simple. Be honest. But most of all be yourself." He leaned back in his chair, expecting the worst, resigned to five more minutes of silly mouthings and posturings.

"Right! I got you!" Ralph took off his voluminous overcoat and threw it down. Then, pulling a chair up to him, he climbed on it and stood as tall as he could.

"I'm God, see?" he called down to Farrell. "And I'm talkin' to this angel, givin' him the business of the day. That's why I'm standin' on this chair, because I'm God. And God is Puerto Rican and he works in a steambath, see . . . and the angel is a computer, an electronic computer . . ."

Al Farrell grunted in surprise. What weird circumstances could have led this boy to Bruce Jay Friedman's play *Steambath?* He felt his attention being pulled to the stage by the energy of this boy, an incandescent, febrile energy that lit up his skinny body and gave him a stature, a presence seen only rarely, and almost never in anybody that young.

"Hiya, baby . . ." Garcia was saying. "San Diego Freeway. I'm still God, right? All right, first thing I want that Pontiac moving south past Hermosa Beach to crash into the light blue El Dorado coming the other way. Make it a head-on collision. No survivors . . ."

Voice all wrong, and movements too jerky, judged Farrell. But those things were correctable. With practice, with training . . .

"Now here's the one I like," "God" continued. "The screenwriter flying out to Beverly Hills. Coming on with the broads. Here's what happens. Over Denver, a stewardess throws a dart in his eye. No doctor on board. He has to go all the way to Los Angeles like that . . ."

The energy was there, frenetic, kinetic. Not a calm, steady wave, but in short, staccato bursts of light and sound. This boy was a pinwheel of emotions, crude but brilliant.

"Now, the producer up in New Haven. Never had a hit. Doing a seven hundred and fifty thousand musical . . . the whole show depends on the female star. All right. A police dog gets loose and bites her tits off. The understudy is scared stiff, but she goes on anyway. Bombsville . . ."

But would he work? Did this boy possess the discipline to put in four years of grueling work here, to do

45

repetitious exercises whose meaning he probably wouldn't understand for a long time? Garcia talked about Freddie . . . did he want to be like him, a rocket that went up in a blaze and fell to earth soon after, its flame extinguished? This was not the school for the Freddie Prinzes of this world, the unhappy clowns doomed to brief, tragic lives and bloody endings. Performing Arts meant hard work and discipline, not showboating and pyrotechnics. The accent here was on group, not genius.

Troubled, Mr. Farrell watched Raul Garcia bring the speech to an end. Would he be doing the kid a favor by admitting him? Or would it be more of a favor to keep him out? The boy seemed so vulnerable; even his attempt at Americanizing his name was an expression of insecurity. There was about him the undefinable aura of the loner. Was he genuinely gifted or did his talent appear only in spurts? In or out? Farrell couldn't make up his mind. In or out?

Ralph thought of the quote. Garcia, he told himself. How can they turn down Garcia?

Leroy Johnson sauntered down the corridor, holding a green slip casually between his long fingers. Shirley had to trot to keep up with him; her short, heavy legs couldn't match his strides. Anger rode her brow, and the corners of her mouth were pulled down in bitterness.

"You're not into high school, remember?"

Leroy shrugged. "I'm thinkin' about it. Anyway, I'm into dancin'."

A short sour laugh escaped Shirley's lips. "You're into chicks, you mean. You don't have to go to no high school for that. Who asked you to work my audition, anyway?"

"You did. I was doing you a favor, remember?"

"Some fat favor." Shirley's lips trembled, but she tried to hide it in angry bravado.

The student monitor at the stairwell took Leroy's slip. "Third floor, please," she told him. "Give your forms to the senior on the door." Glancing at Shirley's yellow slip, she said, "First floor. You can take your things and change in the girls' room. You can wait for your friend on one of the chairs at the back."

It took a few seconds for the penny to drop. "I'm through?" asked Shirley on a rising note. "I don't have to dance anymore? Where you going, Leroy? What's he going upstairs for?"

Leroy didn't answer, and the monitor merely shrugged.

But light was beginning to dawn in Shirley's brain. "Oh, I get it, you think I'm stupid or something? He's in and I'm out, right? He gets to be a finalist and I get the ticket home. The hell with you, Leroy! This was *my* audition. You ain't *into* high school, you mother, this was *my* audition."

With a goodbye smile, Leroy headed up the stairs. Shirley clenched her fists into tight balls and screamed up after him. "We was rehearsin' to get *me* into this school, not *you!* You bastard! It's not fair." Tears welled up in her eyes and began to roll down her glossy cheeks. Slowly, she headed down the stairs to the outside world, leaving behind her all her hopes for Performing Arts. But she wasn't going out sniveling. Not her.

"Now don't get me wrong," she yelled up the stairs. "I didn't want to come here anyway. This school sucks. You done me a favor, Leroy, you louse. You gone and saved me four long years at this dumbass school!" She stopped on the landing and looked up the stairs. Leroy was nowhere in sight. Now the tears poured out of her eyes unchecked, but she still had the energy for one last defiance.

"You lookin' at one happy lady!" she sobbed. "One happy lady!"

"Do you have any more outlets here?" asked Bruno. He held up a tangle of wires, plugs and jack-plugs that had not yet been connected.

Mr. Shorofsky stared at him in amazement. He had stood by speechless as the Martelli brothers had lugged in and set up the heavy equipment, Bruno hovering over it like a mother cat watching strangers handling her kittens. He hadn't said a word as Bruno took fully ten minutes to unroll the cables of wire and make his connections. Every now and then, Shorofsky would sneak a glance at Mrs. Tossoff, who sat shaking her head in stupefaction.

Now the equipment was set up and, presumably, ready to go. Shorofsky eyed it dubiously. The large synthesizer dominated the three keyboards, which in their turn dwarfed the heavy speakers and the amps and pre-amps. Wires coiled everywhere underfoot; Shorofsky was convinced they were a hazard to mortal life and limb. Do you need a license to operate this thing?

"Does he want to be a musician or an airline pilot?" Shorofsky demanded of Mrs. Tossoff, who replied with a European shrug.

"Okay, Mr. . . ." he looked down at his clipboard, ". . . Martelli, we're ready when you are."

Bruno nodded and raised his hands above the keyboards. Out of the speakers came a swelling flood of orchestral sounds—strings, horns, reeds, percussion. The mighty synthesizer was working its electronic miracles on Tchaikovsky.

Shorofsky's grizzled brows shot upward and his glasses slid down his nose.

"Mr. Martelli . . ."

Lost in the surge of the music, the boy couldn't hear. His fingers continued to create thunder and lightning from the keys.

"Mr. *Martelli!*"

Bruno bent his head closer to the roar of the "instruments." On his face was an expression of bliss.

"MR. MARTELLI!!"

Bruno opened his eyes and took his hands off the keys. He looked up expectantly at the old music teacher, who sighed painfully.

"Mr. Martelli. One instrument at a time will be sufficient."

Bruno shrugged in surprise. One instrument, when you could have an entire symphony orchestra! Well, if that was what the old guy wanted . . . He turned off switches, and clicked dials.

"I can do it in five-four if you prefer it with a disco beat," he offered.

Shorofsky shook his head very slowly, as though it ached badly. It did. Taking his glasses off, he rubbed at the painful spots around his eyes and on his temples as the boy finished playing. There was no mistaking it, not even in the artificially amplified sounds of the electronic speakers. The boy's technique and musical sense were excellent; he was a musician born. But all this gadgetry! What was wrong with a piano or a violin? Or a viola, Mr. Shorofsky's own instrument, his darling favorite. All this mechanical nonsense—he waved one gnarled, impatient hand at seven thousand dollars' worth of state-of-the-art engineering.

Grudgingly, the music teacher gave Bruno Martelli the obligatory sight-reading test. It was a brief, intricate Bach toccata that had already sent twenty or thirty boys and girls crashing in flames this very day. But Bruno didn't turn a hair of his curly head. Propping the music up on his keyboard, he played it through without a single mistake.

"Are you sure you've never studied that piece before?" Shorofsky asked suspiciously when Bruno had finished.

"Maybe I heard it," shrugged Bruno casually. "My father's into that kind of stuff."

"What kind of stuff?"

"Moldy oldies. Bach. Puccini . . . all those old guys." He dismissed nearly four centuries of classical music with one wave of his hand. "Now, do you want to hear some real music?" He smiled. Then he flexed his fingers, clicked some switches, turned some dials, pressed some buttons and bent over the keyboard. A solid wall of electric rock went up brick by noisy brick. Bruno's own music; it was enough to deafen a statue.

Shorofsky gritted his teeth in pain. What a pity this boy was so talented! He'd love to boot him out of here, him and his two tons of crazy wires and control panels. Oh, how he ached to reject him. But he couldn't. The boy possessed sure talent and possible genius. Holding his hands over his ears, Shorofsky vowed to pay him back when he got this Bruno Martelli into music theory class.

———————

The long day was drawing to an end. The dancers had packed up their leotards and ballet slippers and left the cavernous dance room to echoes. Under the last couple of lights, Miss Berg attacked her paperwork, sorting out the applications of students she *must* have from others who would fill in the gaps, who were trainable and who moved well and showed devotion to discipline. Leroy Johnson's application lay on top of the pile. It was scrawled in pencil and close to illegible.

Al Farrell had called the drama finalists together to explain that there were more of them, including the finalists from the previous two audition days, than there were places in the school, and that some of them would make it and some would not, but that they would be informed shortly, by mail or by phone.

I won't make it, thought Doris sadly. Everybody here is more talented or more interesting than me.

"We'll make it, we'll make it," muttered Mrs. Finsecker at the back of the auditorium.

I gotta make it, thought Ralph Garcy, no longer God. This was Freddie's school. He would want me to make it. Wouldn't you, Freddie?

Whether I make it or not, I'll have to deal with it, thought Montgomery MacNeill. I'll have to work it out.

"Did ya make it?" Angelo yelled excitedly as he and Mario came to pick up the equipment.

"I don't know yet, but I think so," said Bruno, a little shyly.

"Whaddya mean, ya think so!" demanded Angelo, grabbing his son up in an affectionate bear hug. "Of *course* ya made it."

"Listen," Uncle Mario interrupted as he reluctantly shouldered his end of the heavy synthesizer. "If he doesn't make it, buy him an accordion and let him carry it himself."

I made it, I made it, exulted Coco Hernandez as she rode uptown on the D train. They loved me. Didn't they? Now the only question is: which department accepted me? Music or dance? And when the hell are they going to let me know? Wow, do I really have to wait until next September to start? I wanna be a star. A Star! Now! I want fortune! And *fame!*

FRESHMAN YEAR

1

DORIS came out of the BMT at Times Square and took a deep breath. The sudden, overwhelming fumes of automobile and bus exhausts combined with the smells of hot, rancid grease from the sleazy fast-food joints to almost knock her over. But she didn't mind. She grinned as she almost ran the four blocks to 46th Street. She couldn't wait to get there. To start her new life.

She was still surprised that she'd made it. Actually, she had come so very close to not getting into P.A. at all. She had been chosen third alternate. That meant that three of the people selected on the first list for the drama department would have to drop out before she could get in. And who in his right mind would drop out of Performing Arts? So she had spent the months from last December to this August convinced that she'd have to go to high school in Brooklyn, loathing the idea of it, but helpless in the face of things. What she never took into account was that there were more factors involved in dropping out than mere volition. By August, two of the chosen had moved away with their families, out of New York; the third had broken her leg. And Doris Finsecker had been notified by telephone that she was accepted as a freshman at the High School of Performing Arts for the semester to begin in September.

As she headed east on 46th Street to the school building, Doris slowed her pace. A wave of shyness overtook her when she saw the boys and girls milling toward the school from all directions. She didn't know anybody; not one face, black or white, was familiar to her. It had taken all of Doris's powers of persuasion, which weren't many, to convince Mrs. Finsecker to stay home today. Mrs. Finsecker had accompanied Doris to school on the first day every year from nursery school through junior high, and she wasn't ready to abdicate yet. As it was, Doris had had to listen to twenty minutes of do's and don'ts (especially don'ts) before she was allowed out of the house. A good, hot nourishing breakfast churned in her stomach and made her a little train-sick.

Walking as slowly as possible, clutching her notebook and a useless envelope of eight-by-ten glossies against her thin chest, Doris checked out the other students, especially the girls. It was just what she'd been afraid of. She was dressed wrong. All wrong. She was wearing a cardigan sweater over a pleated skirt, and her hair was tied back from her face in ribbons. I look like Little Miss Muffet, she thought sadly. All I need is a bowl of curds and whey, and a spider.

Around her, bevies of adolescent girls ran by, in pairs and in groups, calling greetings to the boys. Almost all of them wore new jeans, snugly fitted to their budding behinds. And there seemed to be only one way to wear them—with high-heeled boots. If the boots came up high enough, you tucked the jeans—as tight in the legs as you could pull yourself into—down into the boots. If the boots were cut low, you rolled up the pants legs into a broad cuff just above the boot tops. No other outfit would do.

All the jeans Doris owned were full-cut and faded—two no-no's this year—and the label on them was J. C. Penney. The only boots she owned were flat-heeled and lined with fake fur, for snowstorms.

Her hair was all wrong, too. Pulled back off the face and tied up with ribbons had gone out with Shirley Temple. Braids were in, braids twisted around feathers, peeping here and there out from the hair worn loose, straight or kinky, it didn't matter. Some girls sported one braid, some twenty. One tall and languorous black girl had a white gardenia tucked into the braid behind her right ear, a young Billie Holiday. Doris felt very left out, and it was small consolation to know that these fashions would not be seen in Brooklyn for at least another year. She was feeling like an "I Love Lucy" rerun on a ten-inch black and white screen—drab and smaller than life.

For Montgomery MacNeill, the school was a five-minute walk from where he lived, right on Times Square. In fact, you could see from the window of his apartment the statue of George M. Cohan, who wrote "Give My Regards to Broadway." It was only a matter of walking down Broadway, past the junkies, the whores and the pimps, the plainclothes cops sitting in their unmarked cars, the peddlers and the gamblers with their fixed games of "chance" and their shills. On the side streets were bunched the legitimate theatres, their marquees carrying illustrious names. The Shubert. The Helen Hayes. The Brooks Atkinson. Montgomery had grown up in those theatres, on these filthy streets. He neither hated them nor loved them. He accepted them, and had long ago come to terms with the fact that his destiny would probably always lie in these streets, for better or for worse. Making a wide circle around a vicious brawl between a flashily dressed pimp and a knife-wielding prostitute, Montgomery walked south to 46th Street.

Coco Hernandez loved this part of town; it turned her on. *Broadway*, man! That's where they put your name up in lights. And Broadway was only a stepping-stone to Hollywood, where you really achieved stardom. And she was on her way now. She'd gotten up real early this morning, so that she could have her breakfast in the HoJo on Times Square. Having purchased *Show Business* and *Backstage* she'd settled down at a window table to devour two doughnuts and the trade news. The comings and goings of the famous and powerful occupied her attention for three quarters of an hour, and she was still dazzled by big names and bigger deals as she stepped out of the Howard Johnson's. Wow, she was gonna be late on her first day! Better shake that thing and get to school or sure as shit she'd be in trouble. If there was one thing Coco Hernandez didn't need on her meteoric rise to fame, it was trouble. She hitched her new skin-tight jeans up at the waist and tucked the bottoms more firmly into her skintight boots. Then, long braids bobbing, she skidded across Broadway on her high heels.

Bruno sat silent in the back seat of his father's Checker cab. He was, as usual, thinking in music. Most people he knew thought in English, a handful in Italian, but Bruno was the only person he knew of who thought in music. Music occupied his days and his nights—practically his every waking moment. He ate and drank music, took it to bed with him at night and woke up with it in the morning. It was his own music, melodies and intricate harmonies he worked out in his head and tried out on his keyboards in the basement of his father's house in Queens. He'd spent so many hours there, with the headphones on, playing music that only he could hear. Silent music.

Angelo kept watching him in the rearview mirror, but Bruno didn't notice. Damn kid has the headphones on again. He could wear them even when he wasn't wearing them. Wasn't that a pisser? "You okay back there?" he called.

Bruno didn't answer. He wasn't listening.

Tuned in to that music of his. Angelo shook his head, half in worry, half in admiration. That kid had the most single-track mind of anyone he'd ever met. Hey, 46th Street. Nearly passed it. He eased the big Checker east and pulled it up to the curb, right in front of the school.

59

"Here y'are. Signed, sealed and delivered," he joked.

Silence from the back seat, then Bruno slowly opened his blue eyes and looked around him.

"Are we here?" he asked. "Already?"

Already! An hour's drive, and this he calls already. Angelo made a silent appeal to the Virgin Mary, who stood, in plastic replica, on the dashboard of the cab. Then, as Bruno scrambled out, his father pressed a handful of dollar bills into the boy's hand.

"Be good, kid, and knock 'em dead."

Bruno ducked his head shyly. "Thanks, Pop."

Angelo watched him disappear into the school building. It better be worth it, he thought. It damn well better be worth it.

As the taxi pulled away from the curb, a Trans-Am, garishly painted with red and yellow flames, eased into its place. Without bothering to open the door, Leroy hopped out of the car. It was a convertible, and the top was down on this hot September day. He paused for a moment on the sidewalk and grinned, cool in his new vines, a bright leather jacket cut close to his body, his long hair braided tightly in careful cornrows.

"You crazy, man! Watchoo wanna go to school for, man?"

Leroy turned. His friends in the Trans-Am, five boys roughly his own age, were hooting and calling at him. Leroy said nothing, but spread his hands and threw an expressive look at the clusters of bright, pretty black girls crowding into the building. Foxy ladies, his grin said, and all mine.

Now the man was signifyin'. "We hear you," yelled

60

the driver of the convertible, banging on his horn. "Hey, hey," the boys called out to the prettiest of the girls. "Hey, watchoo be callin' yo' sweet little self?"

Leroy shook his head and, shouldering his huge radio, made his way up the steps and into the school.

"Martelli, Bruno."

"Here."

"Hernandez, Coco."

"Here."

"Garcia, Raul." No answer. "Garcia, Raul," repeated Mrs. Sherwood, louder this time.

"It's Ralph," called Ralph. He was being a little slow on the uptake, because he was still stoned from the last joint he'd sneaked before the bell rang.

Mrs. Sherwood checked her attendance card. "It says Raul," she said quietly.

Ralph shrugged. "I don't relate to that." He smiled.

Mrs. Sherwood tapped the homeroom attendance card for a moment. Then she took up a pencil and made a neat correction. "Garcia, Ralph," she called again.

"Garcy," said Ralph, his smile broadening. Hearing snickers coming from all sides of the classroom, he leaned back in his chair expansively, enjoying the attention, basking in the laughter. "They spelled it wrong on the application forms," he explained.

Mrs. Sherwood shot him a sarcastic glance, but she'd had long experience with young actors. Every term, a number of them changed their names to something that sounded less ethnic and, to the kids, more glamorous. She corrected the card a second time.

"Garcy, Ralph."

"Here." The boy beamed.

With a small nod, Mrs. Sherwood continued calling the roll.

"MacNeill, Montgomery."

"Here." This was a quiet boy with a sensitive mouth and a mop of curly red hair. Mrs. Sherwood anticipated no trouble from him.

"Monroe, Lisa."

"Yes?" Lisa had been caught in the act of peering into a tiny pocket mirror and refreshing her lip gloss with her pinkie. Mrs. Sherwood eyed her with mild contempt. Pretty, rather empty, all surface and no depth. Coasting through life on a pass. Sherwood had little use for the breed.

"Johnson, Leroy."

There was no answer. Mrs. Sherwood looked up and scanned the classroom. "Johnson, Leroy!" Silence met her. She stood up and took a good look around. Five seats back she spotted a boy who, her instincts told her, had to be Johnson, Leroy.

The boy sat slumped in his seat, eyes closed, gently smiling. Over his ears, shutting out the real world, was a pair of professional earmuff-type headphones. On his lap was a twenty-five-pound monument to Japanese engineering. Powered by an automobile battery, this suitcase-sized stereo radio/cassette recorder put out enough wattage to run a local radio station. It possessed eight switches, four buttons, four control knobs, directional two-way speakers, a short-wave band, three vu-meters, a number of microphone jacks and lights, controls and swiveling microphones. It cost $345 in the stores and $60 hot in an after-hours club on 125th Street and Lenox Avenue. It minded the baby, did the dishes, tucked you in and kissed you goodnight. And, from the look on the boy's face and the rhythm to which his head was bobbing, it was feeding Donna Summer to Johnson, Leroy in great, loud, creamy earfuls.

Her mouth set in a straight, angry line, Mrs. Sherwood glared down at Leroy. Although she didn't actually remember the knife episode from the last day of auditions last year, a thin unpleasant glimmer of recognition added to her annoyance. As Leroy, oblivious to everything except the disco music being pumped directly into his central nervous system, didn't respond to her, Mrs. Sherwood's irritation grew.

The girl sitting next to Leroy gave him a sharp nudge, and he opened his eyes and lifted one earphone reluctantly.

Standing before him, her narrow face angry, was a tall, thin white woman maybe forty-five years old. He knew the type. Hassle City; she didn't know how to leave a man in peace. He wasn't hittin' on her; why was she hittin' on him?

"Mr. Johnson, in future I'd like you to leave your ghetto blaster at home, please." She cast a withering look at the giant radio.

Leroy didn't deign to raise his eyes. "I brought it in the event of being bored," he drawled.

With difficulty, Barbara Sherwood held on to her temper. To lose it was to admit defeat. "This is a classroom, Mr. Johnson," she snapped. "You're going to be in the same classroom for the next four years with your eyes open, your homework done, your pencils sharpened and all food, cigarettes and radios outside. Do you understand?"

Woman and boy glared at each other for a long moment. Then Leroy angrily snatched the headphones off and stuffed them into his bag. As he did, the earphone jack pulled out and the insistent disco blared into the classroom. Leroy punched at the off button until the radio was silenced.

But Mrs. Sherwood wasn't satisfied. "I'm waiting for an answer."

"I ain't into answers," mumbled Leroy sullenly.

Taking a step back, the teacher folded her arms and looked hard at the boy. "Why are you here, Mr. Johnson?" she inquired in a voice of iron.

Leroy grinned cockily. " 'Cause I'm young and single and loves to mingle," he cracked, cutting his eyes at the prettiest girls around him.

"Speak English," barked Sherwood.

Stung, Leroy shouted back at her, "I speaks like I likes."

"This is *my* homeroom," said Sherwood. "You'll speak as *I* like. I teach English. If that's a foreign language, you'll learn it." She looked around the classroom. This first-day confrontation was giving her an opportunity to make an important point, and she took it.

"This is no Mickey Mouse school," she told the forty-two boys and girls who sat silent before her. "You're not getting off easy because you're talented. You'll work twice as hard. I don't care how well you dance . . ." she flicked a glance at Leroy, ". . . or how cute you are . . ." her eyes found Ralph, ". . . or

64

how many colored tutus you have . . ." Lisa blushed under her look, "if you don't give your academic subjects equal time, *you're out!*"

Walking back to her desk, Mrs. Sherwood picked up the pointer and turned to the blackboard behind her. "There's a new word on the blackboard," she said with less vehemence. "There will be a new word every day. We'll define it and then you'll use it in a sentence. The word for today is . . . *tyranny*. Tyranny: a government in which absolute power is vested in a single ruler." Smiling slightly, Mrs. Sherwood paused to let the message sink in. From the muffled groans and a barely stifled curse from Leroy Johnson, she could tell that it had.

The difference between the High School of Performing Arts and other academic high schools in New York City is that at P.A. you spend half your day working in your department—drama, music or dance. The other half of the day is given over to academic subjects, and the third half is spent in practicing, rehearsing, practicing, exercises and more practicing. That gives you three halves, which is impossible, and that doesn't include homework, term papers, exams, studying or working up dramatic, musical or dance presentations to perform in class. It doesn't leave more than fifteen minutes for a home life or a social life. P.A. is obviously not a school for the lazy, the undisciplined or the undedicated.

Talent, somebody said, is a matter of luck, of being

in the right place at the right time. There's some truth to that, but if you look at it more closely, it turns out to be something like this: luck is a matter of being in the right place at the right time *and fully prepared.* The "overnight sensation" has usually sweated for years to become sensational, and the harder he works, the luckier he gets.

You are born with talent, but skill has to be learned, and a craft takes a long, hard apprenticeship.

This was Al Farrell's thirteenth freshman class, but he approached it with all the eagerness he had lavished on his first. And with a great deal more experience and wisdom.

"Acting," he said with quiet emphasis, "is the hardest profession in the world. Fifty thousand people are walking around calling themselves actors and maybe only five hundred are making a living at it." He looked around the small auditorium while the statistic took effect on his listeners. "And most of those do commercials to pay the rent. The rest wait tables and clean apartments . . . and live off welfare and hope." He saw Montgomery MacNeill nod solemnly and Doris Finsecker bite her lip unhappily. He'd have to break her of that habit.

"And don't kid yourself that talent will get you through," continued Farrell, with a sharp glance at Ralph Garcy, who appeared not to be listening. "You have to have a solid technique, a good agent and most of all a thick skin because you're part of an underprivileged minority. You're going to have to suffer the indignity of cattle calls, rejection, humiliation. For every job there are a hundred smiling résumés thrown in the basket. And you'd better like yourself a lot, because that's all you've got to work with. Use yourself. Your body. Your voice. Your experience. That's what the work of the first two years is about. Playing close to self. Finding out who *you* are, what experiences you've accumulated that you can use to create honest moments onstage."

Ralph Garcy leaned over and put his arm around the cute chickie sitting next to him.

"You wanna accumulate some experience?" he whispered in her ear.

Doris Finsecker gasped in surprise. She had been so deeply absorbed in what Mr. Farrell was telling them that she'd been totally unaware of who was sitting next to her. Now she saw, as she pulled away from his arm, that it was Ralph Garcy, the crude, brash Puerto Rican boy from her homeroom.

"I got experiences to spare," he leered.

Doris stared at him blankly. What on earth could he be talking about?

"I live with two chicks," he bragged, winking.

Shocked, Doris turned her face away from Ralph and stared at the floor.

"That's a dynamite floor," he teased. He moved his head down next to hers and stared into her face with an impudent grin. Trying to avoid him, Doris turned to the wall.

"Hello, wall. You like walls?" Ralph was relentless.

In an agony of shyness, Doris got up and changed her seat. Please, don't let anybody look at me! Embarrassment colored her cheeks a bright pink as she sank into her new seat and tried to listen to Mr. Farrell through the pounding in her ears.

"Start being aware of your feelings and reactions,"

he was saying. "So you can draw upon them when necessary."

In the front row, one boy and two girls took solemn notes.

As serious as Bruno Martelli was about his music, he could never match the solemnity with which Mr. Shorofsky attacked the study program. He brought with him more than sixty years of dedication to the art, and he was advanced enough in age to know that time was the one thing too precious to be wasted.

Bruno groaned inwardly as he sat with the other freshman music students listening to Shorofsky outline what was expected of him.

". . . For ensembles, we must have more violins, so everyone must minor in strings. This is so we have good orchestras for assemblies and concerts. And then you have sight-singing and melodic dictation, theory, keyboard harmony and elementary piano and piano literature . . ." here he took a breath to shove his glasses up on his nose, ". . . and then you have music history and music appreciation, orchestration, dance band and symphonic band, and ensembles . . ."

"When do we have lunch?" called out a boy two seats behind Bruno.

"Eleven-thirty," replied Mr. Shorofsky, who had no sense of humor. "One half hour. And then you have everything else."

"What's everything else?" asked the girl on Bruno's right.

"Biology. Chemistry. Algebra." Shorofsky ticked the subjects off on his ancient fingers. "English. French. Physics. History . . ."

"Do we get to sleep?" Bruno wanted to know.

A few scattered laughs made Shorofsky sigh and put down his notes. It was the same every year. It would take months before these young people, dedicated though they were, accepted the harsh regimen of Performing Arts, before they settled down into the grinding routine of study and practice. After all, they were only fourteen years old, high school freshmen. But they would have to learn.

"Music is the hardest profession in the world," he told them emphatically. "You have to give up something . . ."

"Dance is the hardest department in the school," said Miss Berg with a vehement nod. Around her on the floor of the vast dance room sat her freshman dance students, the girls outnumbering the boys by a ratio of six to one. "You have to arrive earlier to get dressed and warmed up. You'll have to take outside classes in your major field and study ballet, modern, folk, tap, jazz and historical dance here. Not to mention dance history, supported adagio, variation class, makeup, hairstyling, even acting for dancers."

Leroy Johnson pursed his lips in a snort of contempt. When was this skinny white chick gonna cut all this jive mumbo jumbo and turn the music on?

"In addition to dealing with the usual dancers' complaints," Miss Berg continued, "pulled tendons, shin splints, swollen toes, smelly tights and stiff competition, you'll have to keep your academic average well up. So I hope your fathers and mothers and well-meaning gym teachers haven't sent you here with any illusions. Dancing isn't a way of getting through school. It's a way of life plus school. And the school part is easier. You can fail French or geometry and make it up at night or in summer school. But if you flunk a dance class, you're out. Any questions?"

Phenicia rose to her feet. She was a tall, thin brown-skinned girl with a gold ring hooped through one nostril.

"I came here to express the exploitation of underprivileged minorities through the medium of modern dance," she announced in a clear, cold voice.

"Sure," said Miss Berg, unperturbable. "What's your question?"

"Just how much racist, classical stuff do I have to take?" demanded Phenicia scornfully.

"You mean ballet?" Miss Berg's thick black brows arched higher.

"I mean ballet."

"Four years, dear," said the dance teacher briskly. "The first year you'll do a little of everything. Next year, we'll decide your major. If it's modern dance, you'll minor in ballet. If it's ballet, you'll minor in modern. Any other questions?"

Leroy turned to the small, pretty girl seated next to him on the highly varnished floor.

"I ain't wearin' no tights," he told her scornfully.

Coco looked up at him with shy admiration. "You're not?" She pretended to sneak a peek.

Leroy shook his head and the little tails of his cornrow braids bobbed. "I ain't into them. I ain't wearin' no faggot threads. And I ain't doin' no hairstylin', see? And no makeup. An' I ain't havin' to come here early for no warmin' up. I'm warmed up enough." He gave the girl one of his special smiles.

Coco returned the smile with interest. This was one dynamite dude . . . mamacita . . . *look* at those shoulders! "You are?" she purred, arching at him a fraction, just enough to be noticeable.

"I'm hot around the clock," grinned Leroy, beginning to appreciate the appreciation he was getting. He moved a little closer to Coco, and his thigh rested against hers. *All right!*

2

THE incredibly heavy schedule of classes and credits was weighing Doris Finsecker down. No warnings that her mother had ever issued had prepared her for the heft of the responsibilities that P.A. had laid on her. She took her work very seriously, but she'd always managed to keep her grades up without too much difficulty; her natural intelligence, good memory and genuine interest in her schoolwork had put her close to the top of her class through grammar school and junior high. But this! She was certain that Barbra Streisand had never had to face an algebra test on the same day a paper on Stanislavski's *My Life in Art* was due. And some of the body exercises in drama class embarrassed her. She found it almost impossible to shed her inhibitions in a roomful of strangers. She just couldn't let herself go.

As she walked slowly down the corridor to the lunchroom, Doris thought about it. It was hard enough just being a teenager, undergoing bodily changes that were embarrassing to deal with, experiencing thoughts and feelings that were completely new to her. It was hard enough being a high school freshman, expected to struggle with subjects much harder than any in elementary school. It was hard enough trying to squeeze out from under Mrs. Finsecker, who gave Doris no privacy, who wanted to hear every last, tiny detail of Doris's school day. When you put all these pressures together, and added the pressures of becoming an actress—it was a wonder Doris didn't explode. And yet it never occurred to Doris to change her mind, to drop out and go back to an easier life in Brooklyn. It never occurred to her that she wouldn't make it. The school had caught her up in its energy, and although the intensity of it sometimes terrified her, the spell it was weaving held her a contented prisoner most of the time. But how much she longed to be a creator of that energy, not merely its captive!

She had no idea where to begin. Take clothing, for example. At Performing Arts, most individuals set their own styles. The dancers, for example, were seen wandering the corridors in skimpy leotards, sometimes with no more than a jersey wrap skirt covering their tights. They were proud of their spare bodies, so they dressed to reveal the length of their legs and necks. The girls all wanted to look like Miss Berg, anyway, who wore only black. When she moved swiftly and gracefully down the hall, followed by a dozen or more adoring acolytes, she resembled a black swan followed by a troop of crows.

The only jackets and ties in the entire school were worn by a handful of the music students, the classicists. The rest of the school lived in jeans. But what jeans! Tight in the crotch, tight in the behind, French-cut and costing forty dollars a pair. As for tops, imagination ran riot. It would never have occurred to Doris that a printed cotton jacket, from one of the cheapjack stores in Chinatown, would look like a million bucks if belted tightly by a wide sash of purple leather. Yet, the girl coming toward her down the corridor was dressed in one, and she looked sensational. Another girl, a blonde coming out of the washroom, was wearing bright red lipstick and a blouse from the 1940s, with puffed sleeves and little glass hearts for buttons. Her yellow hair was frizzed in World War II style, and it gave her a unique and impish look. Style. Doris sighed. Everybody seemed to have it but her. Doris's mother still chose her clothing, and her idea of suitable school clothing was pleated skirts and loose-fitting sweaters.

And friends. Even though the first year had scarcely begun, most of the kids in her homeroom had already paired off or formed little cliques. They seemed to have so much to talk about! But nobody ever talked to Doris. Nobody, that is, except that Ralph Garcy, and he was so crude, so brash and so . . . shocking . . . that Doris couldn't find anything to say to him. He was a turnoff. Doris longed for a friend, someone she could confide in, someone who might reassure her that these things take time, that style isn't achieved in a day, or popularity in the first semester. Someone to remind her that she was talented, or she wouldn't be here.

Even in assembly, with kids crowded into all the seats around her, Doris had sat alone. Nobody asked her when she was going to get her ears pierced, or whom she was out with last night, or what she was doing after school. Nobody cared. So she sat, among the fourteen- and fifteen-year-olds in the first assembly, watching the juniors and the seniors put on music numbers, or dance pieces, or dramatic readings. She could hardly believe that in a couple of years she might be one of those up on the stage. It seemed to her that she was doomed to freshman year forever.

Sighing with loneliness, Doris opened the lunchroom door.

A wave of noise and heat blasted out of the lunchroom and washed over her, nearly knocking her over. She hesitated on the doorsill, but just as she'd decided not to go in, two eager sophomore girls pushed past her, nudging her into the room. Wide-eyed, Doris took a few steps toward the lunch counter, then stopped. The din was so tremendous, her head was beginning to ring with it. How could anybody stand it?

In red letters the sign said: OCCUPANCY BY MORE THAN 356 PERSONS IS DANGEROUS AND UNLAWFUL, but there must have been at least five hundred kids in the enormous room, which was really two open rooms joined into one. They sat on the chairs, the tables, the windowsills and even the floor. They were stepped on, shoved, yelled at, laughed at, cursed. But nobody appeared to mind. Each was so into his own thing that everyone remained oblivious of the purposeful chaos all around.

Over in a corner, two juniors from the drama department were rehearsing a scene from Molière, in costume, or what passed for costume. In the middle of the room, a cellist was working on a passage from Brahms. Right in front of Doris a dancer tried out a step for her colleagues; by the far wall, another dancer was gluing the bottom of her toe shoe. A noisy game of hearts occupied one long table, accompanied by shouts whenever a card was played or a trick taken. From table to table, kids called to their friends; the groups formed, split up and re-formed with new members, but the ball kept rolling. For every boy or girl who went out the lunchroom door, two seemed to crowd in. And all of this against a constant background of taped music.

Stunned by the decibel level, Doris stood looking for a place where she could eat the sandwich she had brought from home. There wasn't an empty seat—not a chair, not a windowsill, not even a clear patch of floor. The hot-lunch counter was set up against one long wall. A mingling of odors, some tasty, some less so, rose and joined with the sound to form an atmosphere you'd need a power saw to cut through.

Not my scene, thought Doris, and turned to go. But the way to the door was now blocked by a group of black youths with drumsticks and brushes, who had commandeered a table for a drumming contest. Doris looked around desperately for another way out. Five hundred people in this room, and I don't know a single one, she told herself in panic.

Bruno Martelli threw back the cover on one of the two pianos in the lunchroom and played a riff. The box was in tune. Satisfied, he sat on the bench and put both hands on the keys. His music, a kind of progressive rock and roll, poured out of the piano and into the bedlam of the room. But in less than a minute, it had taken command. Toes began to tap; the cello left Brahms behind and began to thunk thunk thunk to the beat. The drummers grinned and took it up. Smiles broke out all around as the dance students stood up and began to move, followed by the other kids. Tables were hastily pushed back to give several hundred boys and girls room to give their bodies to the music.

Coco watched Bruno play, her bright eyes narrowed in thought. He was good. Damn, he was good. He was a professional, like her. She snaked her way through the dancers, with a push here and an elbow there, until she'd made her way to the piano. Sitting down on the bench beside him, she began to play along with him, easily picking up on his beat and improvising variations on his melody line. Bruno turned his head briefly and took a look at her, a skinny black girl. Coco flashed him a grin that lit up her whole face. I can sing, too. And she broke into an improvised lyric that set him laughing. It was about the lunchroom, greasy tacos and the sixty-five-cent daily special that Sadie ladled out of the huge pot on the stove. Maybe it wasn't poetry, but it was fast, funny and original, a hot lunch jam.

Doris Finsecker watched the dancing, wishing she could move in that uninhibited, free-and-easy way. In the midst of the dancers she saw Leroy Johnson from her homeroom, arms raised, eyes closed, slim body twisting in total surrender to the music. He was beau-

77

tiful, she thought. Like something . . . wild . . . and natural.

A tall boy opened the second piano and banged out a few bars in a hard, driving disco beat, a rival to the rock and roll Bruno was playing. "All right!" yelled the drummers, and grabbed the beat, passing it along to the dancers. The gyrations grew wilder . . . dishes flew, chairs and tables were knocked over.

Grinning, Bruno played louder, holding onto his rock and roll rhythms. From the other piano, disco music rose in greater volume, and the lunchroom began to quake in frenzy. Leroy leaped on a table, dancing solo. The girls whipped their long hair around, and even the most dedicated of the classical ballerinas were boogying in their black leotards, kicking out their toe shoes like Rockettes.

The electricity in the room was sparking so brightly it frightened Doris. Gone now was her appreciation of things wild and natural. If there was such a thing as *too* natural, this was it. The sound and the heat assaulted her from all sides, and she pushed her way through the drummers in a kind of hysterical frenzy and made it to the door. On the other side of it, she stood breathing hard, almost gasping, as she waited for the jangling of her nerves to calm down.

"Hi," said a quiet voice.

On the third step from the bottom of the stairwell sat the redheaded boy from drama. He was holding a container of coffee, and swallowing the last bite of his doughnut. "Too wild for you?" he asked, nodding his head toward the lunchroom, which was spilling its mad music into the corridor.

Doris nodded, unable to speak just yet.

78

"Me, too," said the boy. "I'm in your acting class."

"I know," smiled Doris timidly.

The boy held out his hand. "Montgomery MacNeill," he said.

"Doris Finsecker." She shook his hand gravely, then perched on the first step, looking up. "Isn't your mother Marsha MacNeill? The actress?"

Montgomery nodded. He was evidently used to the question. "That's right. Yes."

"She does wonderful work," said Doris enthusiastically.

The boy's thin face lit up with pleasure. "Have you seen her?"

Doris suddenly felt like an idiot. She dropped her eyes, wishing she'd kept her big mouth shut. "Er . . . no . . . but I've heard . . . I didn't know she lived in New York."

Montgomery's face fell. "She doesn't. Well, officially she does, but she's been on the road forever. She gets paid to stay in hotels, but she stays with friends so her per diems all come home to me and Dr. Golden."

"Is Dr. Golden your stepfather?" asked Doris.

The boy shook his head. "No, my analyst."

Doris's eyebrows shot up. She had never heard anybody speak so casually about going to a shrink. "Oh, what's wrong with you?" she asked.

Montgomery shrugged in a matter-of-fact way. "Oh, it's pretty technical," he told her. "I have problems . . . with women."

Doris had no idea what she was expected to say. All that came out was another "Oh."

But Montgomery MacNeill appeared to have lost

interest in the topic. "Would you like to share my locker?" he asked her.

It was something friends did, sharing a locker. It meant that you both knew the combination of the lock, just the two of you. It meant that you'd bump into each other between classes, as you got things out and put other things away. You could even walk there together. Your things were inside—together, yours and your friend's. This boy was asking her to be his friend.

Shyly, Doris nodded yes.

When the dancers took their ten-minute break, Coco Hernandez slipped out of the dance room and up the stairs. When she reached the fifth floor, the music department floor, she slipped out of the stairwell.

"Should you be on this floor?" asked Mrs. Tossoff sternly.

Coco jumped. She hadn't expected a dragon to be guarding the castle. Thinking fast, she smiled politely. "I have a note," she lied. "Miss Berg wants a tambourine."

It worked. Mrs. Tossoff nodded and let her pass. Coco opened the first door she came to and walked into a practice session. Two violin students were working on a duet for strings and insulting each other in a language that sounded like it must be Russian.

"Do you speak English?" she asked.

"How the hell can you go to a New York high school and not speak English?" demanded the taller boy.

"Okay. No sweat. You know Bruno Martelli? A freshman?"

They nodded and pointed impatiently, eager to get back to the duet and the insults.

Coco opened another door, which led to another room and another door, which, when opened, revealed Bruno.

He was sitting at a piano, headphones on his ears. His fingers moved over the keys, but the keyboard was eerily silent. He was totally absorbed in his music; every few bars he would lift his fingers from the keys to make notations on a music sheet propped in front of him.

"Are those music notes?" asked Coco, looking over his shoulder. She'd read a lot of music notes in her day, but none that looked like these.

Bruno looked up, startled. It was the little black girl from the lunchroom, the one who'd played and sung with him. What was she doing here? She wasn't in the music department. She was a dancer. He could tell from her leotards. Removing the headphones, he looked at her expectantly.

"Are those music notes?" asked Coco again.

"No. Laser beams. It's a requiem for Buck Rogers." Bruno never knew what to say to girls.

Coco flashed him a look that plainly said, don't bust my chops. "Oh, great." Then she got right to the point; the dance break was nearly over, and she had to hustle her ass downstairs. "You ever thought of doing some *real* music?" she demanded.

Bruno frowned and stood up. "This *is* real music," he said angrily. "I wrote it. It's *my* music."

Coco scampered after him as he walked away from her. "No, I mean a band."

Bruno shook his dark head decisively. "I don't like bands," he told her shortly. "They crowd me. I prefer my basement—no people."

But Coco was persistent. "Hey, there's a lot of money out there, you know? Like in the summer trade, if we get ourselves together in time." She had one idea in mind, and only one. It was to get ahead. To take every single step along that road that led to fame. And she recognized talent when she saw it. Bruno had it. The cat had magic fingers, and he could write music. What a team they'd make! And, man, could she use the bread!

Bruno remained unconvinced. "No, I'm really not interested."

Coco kept talking fast, pressing. She flashed him her most brilliant smile. "There's tea dances, and parties. Like on Long Island. And weddings . . . and bar mitzvahs . . . and those are steady. You know people are always gettin' married and growin' up."

"I don't want the hassle."

Why couldn't he see? It all seemed so plain to Coco, so logical and practical. "I'll take care of everything," she promised. "Like a regular business manager, you know? I'll look after the bookings, the travel arrangements, the costume designs, for ten percent off the top and then a straight split of the performing cut . . ."

Bruno looked at her closely now. There was a toughness about her that he found himself admiring, a quality of brashness and determination that he didn't seem to possess. Her face was alight with enthusiasm, and her huge dark eyes were shining enormously in her small face. She was really pretty, and he didn't even know her name.

"Costume designs? What costume designs?" he asked despite himself.

Now Coco was in her element. "Nothing fancy, just sequins and stuff, and a see-through something for me, or maybe low-cut. We gotta give them visuals, you know. The sound might be wicked, baby, but when you get right down to it . . . tits book bands." She cocked her head to one side and placed her tiny hands on her hips.

Bruno shook his head and laughed. "I think I'll stay in my basement," he said decisively.

"This is our opportunity! Don't you want success?" demanded Coco.

Bruno fixed his eyes significantly on Coco's flat little chest. "Sure," he said amiably. "I just don't think our tits are up to it." He walked out of the room with a cheery wave of his hand.

Disappointed, Coco kicked the piano. Shit! Some days you couldn't get a break. Now she really had to move to get back to the first floor in time. She didn't want old Ice Berg glaring at her for being late, making her sarcastic remarks. Boy, that bitch could really be cutting. That's 'cause she's the teacher. Big deal. School is just four years o' nothing. Graduating's no Academy Award. Sure, this school is better than *real* school. Like it's free and you don't get raped in the hallways, but it's still small change. I'm just killing time here, Coco told herself as she ran down the stairs. I'm waiting for my Opportunity. Just one big break, that's all I need, not this nickel and dime stuff.

It might be a movie or a Broadway musical, but it's coming! I know it. I keep my eyes open. I read the trades, keep up with the news and the deals and who's doing what. 'Cause me I do the whole thing. Singing, dancing, everything! I'm a triple threat, a born star.

Breathless, she slipped into the dance room just as the freshman girls were taking their turns at the barre. Coco got in line last, and arranged her feet into second position.

Old Mama Rosa, she tells fortunes and she told mine. She says I'm doin' my last dance on this dark little planet. So it's gotta be spectacular. She says how bright our spirits go shooting out into space depends on how much we contributed to the earthly brilliance of *this* world. And I mean to be a major contributor. A sure-as-shit major contributor. No doubt about it.

As she raised her hands over her head, Coco told herself: I'll talk to that Bruno again tomorrow. He'll come around. I saw the way he looked at me. We'll get it together.

Ever since she and Montgomery had become friends, life had become somewhat easier and more pleasant for Doris. She'd never had a close friend before who was a boy and not a boyfriend, but Montgomery had a sweet disposition and a gentle sensitivity that allowed Doris to feel comfortable with him, even to confide in him. He never said or did anything to make Doris think he considered her anything other than a friend, and that suited Doris. It wasn't that she didn't like boys—she did—but Montgomery awakened no such feelings in her, even though he was tall and good looking.

Neither did that Ralph Garcy, although he kept after her with his rude remarks and his knowing leers. Every day he managed to find her somewhere—in class, in homeroom, in the halls—and issue one of his crude and repulsive proposals. Doris, convinced he was teasing her, had learned to ignore him icily. He was just one more petty annoyance.

With Montgomery as her friend, the acting classes had become easier for Doris, even fun. At first, she had found it nearly impossible to laugh and cry on cue, to roar and scream and throw herself to the floor or to do the other body-freeing exercises Mr. Farrell had devised. But Montgomery took these in his stride, and never seemed to feel self-conscious pretending to be an elephant or a tiger or a chair. Slowly, Doris's classroom inhibitions began to dissolve, and she found herself, to her own surprise, looking forward to whatever Mr. Farrell would spring on them next time.

As for Montgomery, although he never talked a lot, he was a very good listener, and he appeared to be genuinely interested in Doris's thoughts and feelings. She knew without being told that she was important to him, and that he counted her friendship as one of the few blessings of his life.

As often as they could, Doris and Montgomery chose each other for scene partners. This went against Mr. Farrell's conviction that the student actor must become part of a group, learn to surrender his identity to the group's and trust the group. But, since Doris appeared to be unfolding like a flower in the sun of Montgomery's friendship, the teacher decided to allow them their close association. For the first year, anyway.

Montgomery was a walking encyclopedia of American and European plays, past and present, so it was always he who selected the scenes for them to work on, and he who "directed" them. Today they were Russian serfs; Montgomery in a shoulder-buttoned blouse, his jeans tucked into his boots, and Doris in a babushka and a wide skirt that mounded over her "pregnant" belly. Under the skirt was a feather pillow Doris had brought from home; it was playing the baby. The scene, from Chekhov, called for them to be thrown off their land a month before the baby was due. They were to sit wailing in the snow. Fortunately for Montgomery, who was a stickler for realism, it had actually snowed the evening before. Unfortunately for Doris, he made her go outside and sit in it.

Doris had to admit that the icy snow under her behind and the frost that bit savagely at her fingers through the holes in her mittens lent an air of conviction to her moans and wails. She was so goddamn cold she *felt* like a Russian serf!

Nobody paid any attention to the pair as they sat on the icy ground in the alleyway behind the school, paperback copies of the play in their laps. Rehearsals were the most common sight at P.A., and they took place everywhere—in the locker room, in the gym, in the lunchrooms, even in the bathrooms. But every now and then Doris's attention would wander to some particularly attractive passing boy or girl—a dancer with long, straight hair flowing, or a senior boy in an ancient raccoon coat to his heels. Finally, at the sight of a petite blond girl who had pasted iridescent stars on her cheeks and temples, Doris threw her book down and buried her face in her hands.

"There's nothing wrong with you," said Montgomery with immediate insight.

Doris raised her face and looked him straight in the eye.

"I know. That's what's wrong with me," she stated plaintively. "Everybody else here is eccentric, or colorful or charismatic. And I'm perfectly ordinary. My nose is ordinary." She gave the offending nose a smack. "My hair is ordinary." She tugged at it angrily. "My body is ordinary. Even my voice is nothing out of the ordinary. I don't know why I'm here."

"You want to be an actress," said Montgomery.

Doris stuck out her lower lip. "Actors and actresses are flamboyant, colorful beings. I'm about as flamboyant as . . . as . . . a bagel," she finished lamely.

"Some people like bagels," said Montgomery mildly. He'd seen this mood before.

At that moment, Michael Lambert, the handsome senior student who had helped Doris through her audition, strolled by, surrounded as usual by adoring young women. Here was the breathing embodiment of the charisma Doris had just been moaning about. Easily, automatically, impartially, Michael flashed Doris one of his famous smiles as he walked on by.

"And some people don't like bagels," she said to Montgomery in a low, sad tone as she watched Michael's progress. Even his *back* had charisma!

"Some people are too old for you," retorted Montgomery.

Doris lifted her chin. "He smiles at me," she said defiantly.

"He smiles at everyone."

"And he winks."

"I think that's a nervous habit."

"And he talks to me. Often," fibbed Doris.

"Oh?" Montgomery looked interested. "What does he say?"

Doris looked down at her mittened hands. " 'Hi,' " she admitted slowly.

"Oh, well," replied Montgomery lightly. "That's serious. Have you set a date?"

Hurt, Doris turned away. Montgomery's face was instantly contrite, and he put his hand gently on her arm.

"I'm sorry," he said softly.

After a minute, Doris turned to him. Her cheeks were scarlet, and twin tears glistened on her lashes. "I feel stupid," she confessed.

"Get into it," said Montgomery briskly. Doris looked at him in surprise.

"Study it. As an acting exercise. The feeling of stupidity. So you can remember it and reproduce it. It might be useful."

Doris nodded slowly, thinking about it. Montgomery was right, as usual. But before she could question him further about technique, Ralph Garcy appeared in the alleyway, dressed, like Dr. Livingstone I presume, in baggy tropical shorts, boots, a pith helmet and binoculars. He made straight for the Russian serfs.

"Hey, M&M," he shouted cheerfully at Montgomery. "You seen your shrink lately?"

"Yesterday," Montgomery admitted.

"You got a special delivery for me?"

Montgomery put his hand in his pocket and pulled out a small pharmacist's bottle, which he handed over to Ralph.

"It's not for me, you know," said Ralph with a mendacious grin, as he whisked the little bottle into his pocket. Then, spying the pillow under Doris's skirt, he gave it a lewd pat.

"How's the floor, Doris? Who's the lucky fellah? Well, what do you know? Somebody finally gave it to old Finsecker. It can't be Gloria here, he's not into chicks." Casting a sly glance at Doris, who was looking puzzled, Ralph clapped one hand over his mouth. "OOOps, shut mah mouth." He danced an elaborate caper, and vanished up the alleyway, the Quaaludes safely in his pocket.

Doris gritted her teeth and shut her eyes tightly in disgust. "I *hate* Ralph Garcy," she growled. "I really do." Then her eyes snapped open. "I must remember this feeling and use it in my acting," she said brightly.

3

AS the first year bumped unevenly along, Leroy Johnson found himself with a set of problems he hadn't expected to have. The idea of getting an education had never entered his mind. Leroy had more or less drifted through the first fifteen years of his life, picking up what he could use. Here and there he had gathered no small amount of street knowledge. He was smart and attractive to girls, and he held the respect of every boy he knew. Somehow or other, he always managed to have coin in his pocket. He wore fine threads, had an active love life—what the hell did he need to read and write for?

But Leroy now found himself hooked on dancing. He never felt so alive as when he came into the large dance room and heard the piano setting the tempo. At first, he'd objected to the exercises and the barre practice and the long warm-ups. After a while, though, his body felt the benefit of the endless practice. He was more limber, could turn faster, jump higher and—almost—fly off the ground, free as air. So he accepted with better grace the need for continual practice, and became a better and more disciplined dancer.

The trouble was that he had to fulfill his academic obligations or he wouldn't be able to continue dancing at P.A. He'd been truant all his school life; now he looked forward to getting to school, to smelling the rosin and the varnish that were the characteristic odors of the dance department, along with the smell of sweat. He liked the kids, too—especially the girls, and of the girls especially Coco, whom he'd begun dating. But apart from dance, everything was a hassle, especially Mrs. Sherwood's English class. It turned out that Leroy had some natural aptitude for mathematics, so algebra wasn't as difficult for him as for others in the class. Biology he would pass, because his lab partner, a small Puerto Rican girl named Lydia, had a crush on him, and did his cell drawings and lent him her homework and notes. But English was a mean mother, potentially Leroy's downfall. He hated the class and he hated Mrs. Sherwood, with her thin-lipped insults and her angry eyes. He was totally bored, and saw no reason to exert himself.

Except there was a reason—dance. If he wanted to dance, he'd have to pass English. So he tried to make an effort, though it caused him more pain than all his other schoolwork lumped together.

His latest hurdle was what Mrs. Sherwood called "a composition." They were supposed to write about their backgrounds, to recall some story about their families which would bear retelling on paper. To Leroy, *family* was a foreign word. He had never known his father, and his mother lived on welfare. She had a severe cough, which she doctored heavily with a syrup containing codeine. She was always stoned and always coughing. From the time he was eight years old, Leroy had looked after himself, coming and going as he pleased. His only brother was in jail for armed robbery. What the hell kind of "composition" could he write about that? The night before it was due, Leroy had scratched out a few paragraphs on lined notebook paper. Miserably spelled and with no punctuation, the composition was about the joys of life on the street in Harlem, its so-called "freedom" and its contempt for middle-class values. This tattered page was the only assignment of the three which Mrs. Sherwood had given the class that he bothered to make a stab at, and only because there was a freshman dance recital scheduled for assembly, and he wanted to dance in it. You couldn't perform if you were incomplete in any of your subjects.

But Bad News Sherwood was far from satisfied. Two days after he'd turned in his pathetic effort, she confronted him in class, demanding—for the third time—Leroy's homework.

"I forgot it," muttered Leroy sullenly.

"For two weeks?" The sarcastic lift to the teacher's eyebrow left Leroy in no doubt about her disbelief.

"I told you I done it and I forgot it!" yelled Leroy defensively.

"My hearing's fine," retorted Mrs. Sherwood. "It's your homework that's missing, and the page that I have is unintelligible."

Leroy felt his cheeks grow hot with shame. He knew the page was bad, but he had simply been unable to do better. "It's a secret language," he mumbled. "It ain't meant for white folks to understand it."

"This isn't a joke," shouted Mrs. Sherwood.

"I got lotsa jokes."

Mrs. Sherwood angrily waved the scribbled paper. "This is *garbage!!*"

The corners of Leroy's mouth went down. "My pen broke."

"It's in pencil."

"That broke too." Nervous laughter rippled through the classroom.

Barbara Sherwood fought to regain her composure. After all, she held all the cards. "If you can't learn to read," she said flatly, "you can't learn to dance. You're flunking out."

Stung, Leroy sat up in his seat. "I can read!"

Mrs. Sherwood stood looking at him expectantly, her eyes challenging him.

"I can read," he said again, less loudly.

"Then read," replied Mrs. Sherwood calmly.

"No!"

"Read!"

"No!" Leroy stole a quick glance around; the rest of the class appeared to be as embarrassed as he was.

"READ!!"

Desperately, Leroy sprang out of his seat and ran for the door. Anger was squeezing him so hard that he could barely choke out words, and fury drove him to kick savagely at Mrs. Sherwood's desk as he passed it. At the door, he turned like a hunted animal at bay.

Tears filled his eyes and his lips drew back from his teeth as he hurled his rage and shame in the face of his pursuer.

"I *can* fucking read, you bigot!" he screamed. "You bitch! I can read!"

Then he threw himself out of the classroom door, hearing—through the pounding in his head—the audible gasp of his classmates and the slam of the door behind him.

Leroy ran down the corridor as though the hounds of hell were barking at his heels. A string of curse words rose to his lips as he ran, and his anger was so great that he felt the need to strike out, to kick and to punch. The worst thing was, it wasn't Mrs. Sherwood he was so angry at, it was himself. He felt a fool—inarticulate, helpless, unmanned. As he ran past the bookcases in the corridor, the sight of the books stacked behind the glass infuriated him. The enemy. Swiftly, without thinking, he lashed out, kicking at the glass until it broke. The sound of the breaking glass unleashed his anger, focusing it on the bookcase. He began tearing at the books and strewing them on the floor, breaking more glass as his rage exploded. Finally he toppled the bookcase to the floor, and watched it shatter into sticks of jagged wood and splinters of glass. But his brief satisfaction turned to fear when he heard the sound of monitors' feet running toward him down the corridor. He turned and fled from the building.

In the classroom Mrs. Sherwood calmly turned to the class and took up the lesson where she'd left off. But inside, her emotions were in a turmoil, and she had to keep biting at her lips so they wouldn't tremble and betray her. Damn that boy! Didn't he have any inkling that she might just be trying to help him? Didn't he know that she was trying to put into his hands the tools he would need to get him through life? It wasn't as though he were stupid; she knew better than that. She herself had a healthy respect for street smarts. Leroy was capable of learning to read, to write, and above all to express himself. She saw no reason for a boy as clever as he was to be crippled by an inability to articulate his wishes, thoughts or needs. He might be fluent in the ghetto, but the ghetto was not the world, and he would need standard English to get by, especially if he hoped to emerge from the ghetto and into the world of dance. It wasn't as if he were lazy; dancers could not afford to be lazy. No, he had simply placed a huge granite block—compounded of "I won't" and "I can't"—between them, and she would need a pressure drill to get through the granite. Very well, then, she'd *be* that pressure drill. Barbara Sherwood was not about to let any student of hers off lightly. Any boy or girl who had the capacity would be filled to the limit with the basic skills life required. Grimly, she forced her mind off Leroy for the present, and back to the rest of the class.

Leroy emerged from the subway station at 116th Street and Lenox Avenue. His mood had changed on the long train ride; he was depressed and, strange to him, a little frightened. The chilly streets echoed his mood; winter held Harlem in its grasp, and the sidewalks—usually crowded with life—were empty and bleak. Patches of dirty snow covered with dog droppings and nameless filth, clung stubbornly to the curbs and made the gutters treacherously slick. Without a destination, Leroy headed east. The tenement buildings and stores gave way to empty lots filled with rotting garbage and rusting metal, playgrounds of the damned. Above his head, the elevated tracks of the New York Central cast gray shadows on the wintry streets below, shadows which lengthened as the short December day drew to an early close.

Leroy climbed the twisted chicken-wire fence of a vacant lot, and aimlessly kicked his way through the garbage. He was chilled to the bone and shivering. He could be indoors now, with a hot cup of coffee. There were lots of places he could go where he would be welcome, but he didn't want to be anywhere. Something was clinging to his foot; Leroy looked down.

A large piece of tattered paper had detached itself from the mound of refuse and wrapped itself around his foot. He kicked it away, but it only clung more tightly, as if it had a purpose. Patiently, Leroy bent and pulled it off. There was printing on it. In the dim light of the closing day, it was hard to make out the words, but Leroy felt driven suddenly by an impulse. He wanted to, needed to, know what it said. He held it up to the fading sky.

"Please . . . read . . . care . . . care . . . carefully," he recited painfully, following each syllable with the tip of his finger. "Wel . . . come to the wonder . . ful . . . world of . . . Maytag . . . washing . . . ma . . . ma . . . machines . . ."

Welcome to the wonderful world of Maytag washing machines. It was a message, in writing, and Leroy had deciphered it. It must have taken him a while, but nobody was on his back, nobody was hassling him, and he had read it. He had *read* it! Suddenly, he knew that it wouldn't be easy, but it would be possible. He sat himself down on the refuse pile, oblivious of his brand-new jeans, and wrapped his arms around himself. His body rocked to and fro in the cold, but Leroy remained there . . . hugging himself tightly, allowing the warm feeling of flickering hope to dissolve the dark shroud of despair.

Unlike Leroy, Bruno found Performing Arts no hassle. Without exerting himself, he managed to keep an 85 average in his academic studies. He did his homework methodically and quickly, just to have it out of the way so that he could spend more time on his music. Every night, after he closed his books and ate his dinner, he went down to the basement and plugged his headphones into the jack. Then he'd seat himself at the keyboards and allow his music to take hold of him. He was writing steadily now.

Contrary to what Mr. Shorofsky believed, Bruno quite enjoyed his music classes—theory, harmony, history and the rest of it. Nothing having to do with music was distasteful to him, even though his idea of what constituted music was very different from the aging professor's. To Shorofsky, music was the harmonious blend of a group of instruments playing in concert, each musician making an individual contribution to the melodious whole. To Bruno, music was one human and many pieces of electronic equipment—the single vision of one pair of hands, one mind, evoking a symphony of sound from machines. Never would they see eye to eye, but Shorofsky grudgingly granted Bruno respect, and Bruno less grudgingly granted it back.

The boy didn't socialize, always leaving school as soon as classes were over. Most of the other boys and girls remained behind for extracurricular activities and clubs, but none of that interested Bruno. He took reluctant part in orchestra rehearsals; there was no way of getting out of them. But nothing else could keep him from his basement studio for an extra hour. Nothing was worth it.

If he'd ever stopped to think about it, Bruno might have admitted that he was sometimes lonely. But he took it in stride. Someday he would probably marry and have children of his own, but he postponed even thinking about that. Someday was very far away. First, there was success. He was confident that it would come. But even success didn't interest him as much as the process of creation, of writing the songs and hearing the music that was born in his brain emerge from his fingers.

Meanwhile, Coco Hernandez, that kook, kept after him night and day. He admired her energy, and the thought of forming a live band didn't seem quite so off-the-wall anymore. He was getting used to having her around. When she missed a day of hounding him, he felt a small, sharp pang of loss he couldn't quite identify. Her star-spangled dreams, all tinsel and glitter and name-up-in-lights, were so different from his own, but her exuberance made him laugh, and he wasn't much given to laughing.

His father insisted on driving him to school every day in the big Checker cab. At first, it made Bruno uncomfortable, but by April he was used to it. Sitting in the back seat, his head resting against the plastic, Bruno would give himself up to new musical ideas. He ran through phrases and bars in his head, discarding what didn't work, replaying over and over the ones with promise. He rarely spoke to his father, and was unaware that his father studied him constantly in his rearview mirror.

Angelo Martelli loved his only son, but he didn't understand him. A love of music ran like the blood through his veins, and the purity of a Verdi opera was to him unparalleled bliss. Yet Angelo was no fool, and he knew that pop music was where the money was made today. Pop stars brought in big bucks; they were the financial elite of the entertainment world. So, when Bruno showed talent early, Angelo had rejoiced and had lavished on his son all that was within reach of his limited resources. He even went into debt; he'd be paying off this last equipment setup for three more years at least. But he considered it an investment in the future. He never doubted that someday it would pay off.

Nor had Bruno disappointed him. He was a good boy; he didn't run around. You could always find him in the same place, down in the basement, hooked up to the keyboards. Music was his life.

But that too was a problem. The boy was close to fifteen years old, tall and handsome like his old man, with the same dark hair and startling blue eyes, but with dimples, too, a gift from his mother. Girls should be falling all over him, but Bruno didn't seem to acknowledge their existence. Handsome kid like that; it wasn't natural.

"It's not natural," he said out loud, with a glance into the rearview mirror.

"Huh?" asked Bruno, roused from his rock and roll reverie.

"You're fifteen years old. It's not natural you never have a date, go out with a pretty girl . . ."

"Get off my case, will ya, Pappa?" begged Bruno. He never knew how to deal with this. It was so . . . so . . . *embarrassing.*

"When *I* was your age," began Angelo Martelli, the usual introduction to the same old song.

"Please!" moaned Bruno, but Angelo was relentless.

"I had girlfriends, lots of girlfriends. I had a different girlfriend every day!"

Bruno sank back on the seat. "I got music," he muttered.

For a minute or two Angelo gave his full attention to the traffic, which as they crossed into Manhattan was bumper to bumper. As another cab cut in front of him, Angelo pounded on his horn, then gave the driver the finger. When the light changed to red, and the Checker came to a halt, Angelo turned to look reproachfully at his son.

"Sure you got music. Okay, but for what? For yourself? For your headset. Do I hear it anymore? Does your mama hear it? Do your friends hear it? Do you have friends?"

Bruno roused himself to answer his father. "I don't have time," he said weakly. "I told you. I don't have time."

Angelo turned back to the wheel. "You told me," he said with a tinge of bitterness. "It's not natural. When I was your age, I'm telling you, I . . ."

"Stop telling me," flared Bruno. "You're not my age. Nobody's my age. Maybe I'm ahead of my time. Maybe I don't think people will like my stuff . . ." This was his deepest secret fear, one that he'd never articulated.

"How do you know what people will like?" demanded Angelo with a Neapolitan lift of his brows. "How do *they* know if they don't hear it? How do they hear it if you don't play it for them? How do they recognize your talent . . . and give you scholarships . . . and record contracts . . . and awards?"

His logic was unanswerable, and it defeated Bruno. He resorted to feeble sarcasm. "Maybe they don't. Maybe I die undiscovered and my ghost gets the Grammys."

Angelo shrugged. "Maybe. Maybe. Maybe. Listen, did I build a studio in the basement for a ghost? Did I spend seven thousand dollars on equipment for a ghost? Does your mama cook and clean and wear old clothes for a ghost? Elton John's mama has six mink coats!" He lapsed into silence, aware that he'd made his strongest point; he had nothing more to add.

Bruno shut his eyes and let the guilt wash over him. Pappa was right, as usual. He had a way of putting his finger directly on the sore. But that didn't make it hurt less.

101

The freshman drama class had progressed from group exercises to individual exercises.

"I want you to observe yourself doing ordinary, everyday things," Mr. Farrell had instructed them. "You'll be asked to duplicate them in class. An actor has to develop an acute sense memory, so concentrate on how you deal with *things* in your world. Watch how you wash your face or hold your fork or lift your cup or comb your hair. Observe and study your own mechanicalness. See if you can catch yourself in the very act of doing something, or saying something. See if your actions and reactions fall into patterns and what those patterns are. In particular, notice the way you deal with the physical world. Isolate and focus on particular details."

Mr. Farrell looked around him. The freshman students stared back at him raptly, eager to accept this new assignment.

It was Doris who got the most out of Mr. Farrell's assignment. She had never analyzed any of her actions—emotional or physical—before, and as she grew more conscious of self she grew less self-conscious. Mirror-gazing was novel to her, and she found it a joy to make faces at herself and watch her features change into new ones as she frowned, smiled, cried, gasped in surprise, alarm, dismay. It was a comfort to know that her face worked, and that she chewed her food not very differently from the rest of the world. It gave her a new sense of freedom, and a little release from the tyranny of shyness. She thought nothing of practicing her facial exercises on the subway going home, even though one or two people were staring at her. Well, let them. Someday they'd pay to stare.

Even Ralph Garcy didn't bug her so much anymore. When they'd brought their physical exercises into class and it was Ralph's turn, he had done so convincing a job of sitting on the pot that everybody, even including Mr. Farrell, had laughed at his grunts and bugged-out eyes. Doris was the last one to get the joke, but instead of blushing at her naiveté, or shrinking in horror from Ralph's vulgarity, she had allowed herself the luxury of a loud laugh. It felt good.

Sometimes you just had to laugh at Ralph, weirdo though he was. His sense of timing was often superb. Montgomery seemed to like Ralph a lot, and little by little Ralph was beginning to spend more time with the two of them. Doris didn't mind as much as she'd expected. Ralph still teased her, but she had learned to shrug it off. Playing cool was part of the new image she was trying to build, along with her new sense of style.

Montgomery MacNeill had never been so happy. His friendship with Doris was the most important thing in his life, next to acting. There was a fresh radiance, a purity about her that spoke to his inner self. She was a good listener, too, always ready with a word of genuine sympathy when he needed one. Now she was in the process of changing—from a child into a young woman, from a timid nothing into a budding actress. The process was thrilling to him, and as she unfolded, seeking the sun, he experienced a feeling of pride at being able to help her find her way. He loved her, truly loved her.

And there was Ralph; what was Montgomery to

make of Ralph? Never were there two more dissimilar people—in attitude, personality, and background—than Montgomery MacNeill and Raul Garcia. Where Montgomery was sensitive and quiet, Ralph was loud, brash and boorish. He was, in his merciless teasing, frequently hurtful. But despite all this, Montgomery found himself liking Ralph. His sense of humor was infectious, his talent for comedy was undeniable, and Montgomery sensed that there were depths to Ralph that were hidden from view. Something sad about him captured Montgomery's imagination. He found himself wondering about Ralph, who he was underneath that bluster, and what he was truly like. Mr. Farrell had stressed again and again that they were to work hard on finding out who they really were. Doris had made great strides in that direction; Montgomery had been working on that very thing, with the aid of Dr. Golden, for years now. But Ralph never seemed to scratch the surface of his own nature. Either he didn't care or, what was probably more true, he didn't want to show his real nature to anybody, including himself. Why?

They had been slaving over the same set of dance exercises all morning, and the class was exhausted. This was the brutal reality that Miss Berg had threatened them with at the beginning of the term. This dreary repetition, up down up down up down, would end inevitably in swollen ankles and toes and grinding aches in every muscle. It was good for them, but it was painful.

As usual, Lisa Monroe had insinuated herself into the back row of dancers, where it would be harder for the teacher to see her. There she bent and stretched with the rest of them, but she bent less deeply and stretched less fully. Once or twice, she bobbed instead of bending and waved one arm instead of stretching. It wasn't exactly cheating—Lisa never thought of it as cheating—it was just a matter of saving her strength for later, more showy exertions.

Lisa was just coming up from a halfhearted bob when she realized with horror that Miss Berg had walked down the ranks of the dancers and was standing next to her, glaring.

"Where's the sweat, Lisa?" she demanded in a voice of iron. "I want to see the sweat."

Lisa had the grace to blush bright pink, but after Miss Berg had stalked away, she made a face at the teacher's back. Old Simon Legree! Who wanted to smell of sweat anyway? Dancing ought to be graceful, a thing of beauty, not all this huffing and puffing. Once more, she allowed the hard work to go on without her, as she marked time until the end of class.

When the bell rang, Coco stood up with a groan. What a workout Miss Berg had given them today! *Madre de Dios*, but she'd be one big charley horse tomorrow! And what about tonight?

As she limped toward the girl students' dressing room, Coco heard a voice calling her name. She turned. Phenicia, tall and cool-looking despite the strenuous exercise, was pushing her way toward Coco.

"Muhammad Anderson is giving a talk tonight on African consciousness. Right after Swahili class."

"I'm sorry, baby, I'm booked," smiled Coco. That crazy Phenicia! If her African consciousness got raised one more notch it would go through the ceiling.

"It doesn't start until seven thirty." You had to hand it to her; the girl was persistent.

Coco shrugged, then her features twisted in a wince. Her foot was killing her! Gratefully, she sank onto a dressing-room bench and eased off her dancing shoes. "I'm helping Leroy with his homework," she told the other girl.

"Spanish lessons," remarked a short black girl.

"He's not into Spanish," put in a tall white girl.

"He will be tonight," laughed the black girl.

Coco looked up from her red, blistered toes and grinned. "He sure will," she promised with a cheerful leer.

But Phenicia hadn't given up yet. She was determined to waken Coco's black conscience. "Tomorrow there's a slide show on 'The Uganda Experience,'" she insisted. The girl was a walking bulletin board.

With a little groan, Coco lowered her foot into a basin of warm water. "Tomorrow's Bruno. Band rehearsals. He's real good. We're gonna be sensational."

"I thought he wasn't interested," said Phenicia, miffed.

Coco shrugged. "He changed his mind." She herself had been taken by surprise when Bruno had approached her weeks ago to say that he was ready to form a band and get some outside work.

"Is *he* into Spanish, too?" purred the tall white dancer.

Coco bent closer to the painful blister, examining it dolefully. "No, this is strictly business," she retorted. Then, half to herself, she added, "I don't go with white boys."

"He plays black."

"Yes," nodded Coco. "But not with me."

The first year was coming to an end. Freshman demons had been conquered; those who had remained in the school now looked back on their September fears and laughed. What babies they'd been! Now they were settling more or less comfortably into the difficult routine, accepting as normal the heavy burdens of work that had staggered them at first. As the weather had grown warm and the days had lengthened, the boys and girls had taken to the out-of-doors. Hanging around the school steps and the fast-food restaurants and small cafes of the neighborhood, they'd formed new friendships, and a few romances had tentatively begun. Leroy and Coco, for example, were together a lot of the time, in school and out of it. Coco's face often wore a look of dazed happiness. Everything was starting to move for her. She had her man, her main man, and she had the band. They'd begun to rehearse already, and Coco was developing her brash manner on the telephone. She hadn't nabbed bookings for them yet, but the sheer force of her persistence in the face of refusals made it only a matter of time. The band wasn't half bad, either, Coco thought. Not with

Bruno on the piano and me on vocals. Coco was certain they'd make a name for themselves on the high school dance circuit, Bruno's Black and White Band Featuring Coco Hernandez. Bruno wasn't so sure. He still found rehearsing with other musicians—even kids his own age—uncomfortable. But he bit the bullet.

As for Doris, she gave little thought to romance, but what little she had was aimed at Michael Lambert. When she thought of him it was with a stab of pain. As a senior, he was leaving this month, headed for stardom and fame. Although Doris knew that she'd never really had a chance with him, deep inside she believed that if only he could have known the real Doris it might have been another story. The real Doris was only beginning to emerge, and it was a cause for sorrow that Michael wouldn't be around to see the caterpillar change into a butterfly.

He still smiled at her, though, whenever he passed her in the hall. And Montgomery was wrong! He *didn't* smile at everybody. Most people, maybe, but not everybody. And someday he would be somebody very important. Would their paths ever cross again, out there in the real world? Tune in tomorrow, that's what Montgomery would have said.

Doris was glad Montgomery wasn't with her now, or she'd never have had the courage to put out one hand and stop Michael as he passed her on the stairs. Automatically, he turned his smile on her, and Doris found it suddenly very difficult to breathe.

"Will you sign my yearbook?" she asked him shyly, her eyes avoiding his.

"Sure."

He was so handsome! Tall and blue-eyed, he had those perfect good looks the magazine models displayed—regular features, cleft chin, thick brown hair precisely hot-combed. As he bent to take Doris's book, a whiff of his after-shave rose to her nostrils. It thrilled her, such a fresh smell of lime, so masculine!

"Congratulations," she managed to say.

"Thanks," said Michael.

"You don't have to thank me." Doris's words tumbled out quickly, she was so afraid she'd lose her nerve. "You deserve the award. And the scholarship. You *are* the best actor in the school. I mean . . . you *were*. I'll . . . I mean . . . we'll miss you."

"And I'll miss you," responded Michael automatically.

Doris drew in her breath. "You will?" Then, attempting to keep her voice casual, she added, "Oh, well, we'll keep in touch, I guess . . ."

But Michael was opening her yearbook, looking for his picture to sign. When he found it, he looked up, a little embarrassed. "I'm sorry . . . I don't remember your name."

"Doris Finsecker," said Doris swiftly, her face reddening. "Doris is enough." After all, why should he remember her *name?* They'd never really spoken together before. "Have you decided where you're going?"

"California," said Michael, handing back the book with another smile.

California? Doris moved quickly after him as he continued his way down the stairs. "I meant college. The scholarship."

"Oh, I can't use it," said Michael over his shoulder. "William Morris has big plans for me. They saw me in the Senior Day show and they want to represent me."

They were on the main floor now, heading for the street, with Doris still tagging after Michael. "Who wouldn't?" she breathed. "I mean, that's wonderful! They're the biggest agents in the business."

Michael gave her a gratified nod, but kept his off-hand manner, Joe Cool. "There are a couple of series they think I'm right for. You know the one with the island and the midget? The midget's getting his own show."

"Really? That's great!" squeaked Doris, but her heart sank. If she ever thought he was above her before . . . he was light-years away from her now, and getting farther off with every minute. "Wow, Hollywood."

"Yeah, well . . . here I go, into the sunset." Michael waved his hand. It was apparent that the conversation was over. He'd had a sufficient dose of adolescent admiration and was ready to move on.

"Good luck!" called Doris to his retreating back. "Er . . . sorry . . . I mean . . ." She searched for the phrase that theatre people use to wish one another luck. "Break a leg!" she yelled. She crossed her fingers for him.

Without turning, he shot her another wave.

"See you at Schwab's!" she hollered after him, then she balled her little fist and struck her forehead with it. Of all the dumb, childish things to say! God, I hope he didn't hear *that*. And thank heaven Montgomery wasn't around. She knew exactly how he'd look at her.

He'd shake his head slowly, in an exaggerated parody of amazement that anybody could be so out of it. And all the while his eyes would tell her she was more to be pitied than censured.

SOPHOMORE YEAR

1

ONE of life's great progressions is the summer that takes you into your sophomore year of high school. Being a freshman is almost not like being in high school at all. You have come from a small pond in which you have grown into a pretty large fish. Now you're back at the bottom of the ladder again, younger and possibly smaller than anyone else in school, unfamiliar with the crucial rituals, hidden signals and precious bits of information that will make you an accepted part of the process. Sometimes you think that you are never going to survive the frustrations of the freshman year.

But the year does end, and following it comes a long and glorious summer in which things happen to you. For one thing, you grow. If you're a girl, the chances are that you're already taller than many of the boys in your class, because girls grow earlier. So the inches you add are not necessarily in height, but you discover that your breasts are growing at last, finally filling out to fit that training bra you've been hopelessly wearing for a year.

If you're a boy, strange things begin to happen to your voice, your face and your body. They are all changing in new and sometimes embarrassing ways. The hair that sprouted last year on your upper lip begins to darken and look more like a moustache than like kitten's fur. Your voice surprises even you as it wanders from a squeak to a deep growl in the same sentence. Over the summer, you've added inches here and there. When you crowd into your first assembly as a sophomore, your old friends will have to look at you twice, to make certain it's really you.

Over the summer you have felt a new set of longings, to go with your new body. Dates, if you have them, take on new, heavier significance. If you're not dating, then you think about it all the time. Will I meet him soon? Is she the one? The body longs to be in love, or, at least, to have its newly ferocious curiosity satisfied.

Since the dawn of time, when the first cave-boy hid behind a boulder to sneak a look at the first cave-girl, boys have been creeping around trying to "see something" that's none of their business. The third-floor boys' toilet at Performing Arts is the perfect case in point. Years and years and years ago, some enterprising student discovered that the boys' bathroom shared a common wall with the outer dressing and undressing room of the girls' john. The heavy insulation that had once wrapped the water pipe that fed both bathrooms had been removed decades ago and never replaced. So, around the pipe where it went through the wall was a space small enough to be unnoticed by the girls and large enough to be looked through by the boys.

Now this was no easy maneuver. A boy had to climb on top of the toilet tank, wriggle up hand over hand through the tangle of heated plumbing and finally hoist himself onto the main pipe. Then, perched precariously, he could put his eye to the opening in the wall, where, if he were very lucky, he might see one or two actresses or dancers taking off their bras.

Granted, you had to be pretty desperate to go through all that hassle just on the chance you might see a half-naked girl. But consider this: the root of the tapioca plant is poisonous; if you eat it in its natural state, you'll die in agony. Yet a South American tribe discovered long ago that if you boil it, and pound it and boil it again, then mash it and lay it out to dry, you can safely eat it. And if humankind can go to all that trouble for tapioca, how relatively minor are the troubles teenage boys will endure for a glimpse of something as important as female flesh.

Little wonder that the third-floor john was a hive of activity after each change of classes. Especially today, the first full day of classes in the new school year. Bringing new girls.

By the time fat Tyrone had huffed and panted his way up the stairs, down the corridor and into the john, three sophomores and a senior were already perched high above the floor, peering lustfully through the cracks. From the enthusiasm in their voices, Tyrone could tell they were drooling.

"She's new," breathed one.

"She's gorgeous," sighed the second.

"Please be in music," prayed the third boy, who was in music.

"Please be an actress," begged the senior, who was in drama.

Evidently, the girl had reached into her bag and pulled out a pair of tights.

"She's a dancer!" cried the first boy.

"Shit!" This was from drama and music.

"I don't know about her tits yet."

Below them, Tyrone was hopping around in an agony of suspense and frustration. "Tits?" he croaked. "What do you see? What kind of tits? Big ones?"

"She's gorgeous, fucking gorgeous," moaned the senior.

"Pointy ones?" Tyrone was being driven mad, obsessed with mammaries.

"She's loaded, too."

"Little Miss Moneybags," commented one of the sophomores glumly.

"Little bitty ones? But cute . . . with little nips like raisins?" Tyrone waved his paws in the air, big circles, small circles, pointy circles . . .

"She came in a white limousine," said the sophomore.

"So what? Who couldn't *come* in a white limousine?" demanded the senior.

"She's gorgeous," breathed the music major again.

This was too much for Tyrone. He had to see for himself, and these guys weren't giving an inch. He scrambled over to the pipes and tried to climb, but fell back in pain.

"Give me the gloves, the pipes are too hot."

A worn pair of workman's gloves, handed down through generations by thousands of nameless boys, was tossed down. Tyrone grabbed them and tackled the pipes again.

This time he made it, puffing from his exertions, his round face a dangerous bright pink. He scrambled his way onto the main water pipe, elbowing the others aside.

"The tits! Where are her tits?" he shrieked desperately.

"Never mind the tits! Look at that ass!" the senior shrieked back.

Unfortunately for generations of boys to come, a sudden silence in the girls' room had made Tyrone's cry entirely audible there. Gasps of horror were followed by loud screams as the girls looked up for the first time, saw the hole in the wall and the sweaty, eager faces of four boys leering at them. Alarmed by the screams, the boys began to scramble away as the girls reached for towels, blouses, anything to cover their nudity. But their balance, never very secure, was totally destroyed by their panic, and down they tumbled, like four Humpty-Dumptys off the wall, Tyrone landing with a squashing sound on the senior's back.

"Ow!"

"Shit!!!"

"Get off me, you fat turkey!"

The school year had officially begun.

The object of all this attention smoothed her long blond hair into place with a cool fingertip, checked to make certain the seams of her tights were straight over her firm buttocks and shouldered her dance bag.

Pathetic cretins. If those feebs wanted to look, why not let them? Hilary Van Doren wasn't ashamed of her supple dancer's body. She didn't care who saw it, as long as they stayed on their own side of the wall. Hilary was accustomed to admiration from inferiors. It went with her icy good looks and her station in life. It went with her education, and her poise, her wardrobe and her talent.

Eight years of exclusive private schools had created in Hilary a first-class, full-time elitist. She was saved from total snobbery only by her innate recognition of excellence in others. This she respected, no matter what form it took. Take, for example, her very presence at the High School of Performing Arts.

Needless to say, her father, who had spent thousands of dollars on Hilary's private school education, and many thousands more on music and dance lessons, not to mention ski school in the Italian Alps, did not want his pampered darling to attend a public high school. It was Hilary's own idea, based on the school's high reputation, and the number of dancers it placed each year with major companies all over America. It had seemed to Hilary that nothing would speed her faster on her way to becoming a prima ballerina than three years at P.A. Coolly, she had auditioned, been accepted to the dance program and registered, all without telling her father, whose signature she had forged on her application and registration forms. Of course, once it was a *fait accompli,* she had informed Daddy-O. Wearily, he had agreed to let her try it.

So here she was, on the west side of Manhattan. It was a long way from Park Avenue, to judge from the noise and the smells. Hilary had never heard such bedlam as this locker room, with its clanging steel doors and its screams of hilarity. Earlier today, in the first-floor entrance area, she had seen boys and girls rehearsing scenes in groups of two, five or a dozen. Some wore outlandish and bizarre costumes, evidently homemade. Each group seemed to be trying to out-shout and outperform all the others. There was one telephone booth on the main floor. Between classes, half the school lined up to use it. It was probably the only telephone booth in all the world where the graffiti consisted of equal parts of John-Loves-Mary, sexual innuendo and the scrawled telephone numbers of talent agencies, casting directors, record companies and booking offices.

Something in this raw, energetic earthiness appealed to Hilary. She was used to polished manners, clean fingernails and subdued conversation. Nothing like this kinetic, raucous, babbling action had ever formed any part of her education; Hilary thought that, contrary to her father's expectations, she was going to like it here.

Miss Berg had accepted her enthusiastically into the sophomore dance class, recognizing that Hilary's talent had been enhanced by many years of private training. So accomplished a dancer, especially a classical dancer, was rare to the department, and the teacher's heart had swelled when she watched this aristocratic girl with her incredibly long legs. A ballerina born.

121

Hilary sailed into the dance room and swept over to the barre, where she began practicing her deep bends as a warm-up exercise. Lisa Monroe spotted her instantly and raced over to take the place behind her at the barre. This new girl possessed such an air of glamour that it drew Lisa to her like a magnet.

"Hi, I'm Lisa Monroe," she announced breathlessly.

The new girl didn't turn around or miss a beat. Her long hair, dark blond with highlights of gold, swept toward the floor as she dipped. "Hilary Van Doren," she said out of the corner of her mouth.

Hilary Van Doren. Wouldn't you just know she'd have an elegant name? Wonder if she made it up? Suddenly, Lisa felt plain, almost dowdy, for all her colored tutus.

"I love your coat," she confided. "I saw it in Bergdorf's window. Or was it Bendel's?"

"My stepmother bought it for me," said the girl wearily.

"I wouldn't mind that kind of stepmother!"

For the first time, Hilary shot a quick look at Lisa. Pretty, but not very confident, she thought. And she can't dance for shit. Look at her, she doesn't even make an effort to get her back straight or her arm into a graceful stretch.

"She didn't do it for *me*," she answered in a tone of scorn. "She wants my father to think she cares. Besides, she loves shopping. She has a multiple orgasm every time she buys something."

"She sounds great. I think I like her."

"You can have her," retorted Hilary coldly, putting her heel up on the bar and bending her head forward to touch her ankle. "I don't want her."

"Where's the sweat, Lisa?" Miss Berg had come up behind Lisa to issue the now familiar refrain.

"I'm working on it," said Lisa defensively.

"You're not working on it hard enough," snapped the teacher, moving away. Boy, she had antennae everywhere. Lisa shrugged and glanced sideways at Hilary, who, with vast unconcern, was going through her ballet positions with practiced grace.

"I started with tap and stuff," confessed Lisa, "but my Mom kept buying me these pretty ballet tutus and I just got hooked on it.

"I'm not naturally graceful," she went on. "Grace doesn't run in my family. It's our genes, I guess. I've had to work very hard to get this far. My God, I've been at it since I was four!"

"Less lip, Monroe, more sweat," called Miss Berg from another part of the room.

Lisa went into a deep forward bend, so Miss Berg wouldn't see that she was still talking. "And it doesn't help when the head of the dance department hates you."

But Miss Berg had sharp eyes and ears. "When I say extensions, Monroe, I don't mean your mouth."

"Sorry, ma'am." Under her breath, Lisa added, "Why don't you shut yours?"

But now Miss Berg's attention was elsewhere. She was coming down hard on Leroy Johnson for wearing his cutoffs on the floor. Dancer's tights were mandatory, but Leroy hated them like poison; he thought they were for sissies, and he wouldn't be caught dead in them.

For the first time, Hilary's attention was drawn

away from practice. She stared openly at Leroy, who was arguing with Miss Berg.

"I got 'em, I just forgot 'em," he was protesting.

Hilary turned to Lisa. "What's he talking about?"

"Tights. He won't wear them."

Hilary looked the boy over appreciatively. *"C'est dommage,"* she murmured. What a pity. That superb body of his would be smashing in tights.

Lisa didn't catch the words. "What's that?"

"French, dear," purred Hilary. Without taking her eyes off Leroy, she added, *"Son derrière noir, c'est formidable."*

"I love your accent. What did you say?"

Hilary smiled slightly. "I said, dear, that I dig his black ass."

Instantly, a small black girl with huge eyes, who'd been working at the barre in front of Hilary, wheeled around glaring. "It's taken, Goldilocks," snapped Coco.

Hilary narrowed her eyes, and her full lips curled in a confident smile: "Don't count on it," she said lightly. Then, before the angry Coco could protest, she danced down the barre like a tall snowflake, coming to a stop beside Leroy.

Coco watched in growing misery as Leroy's sullen look began to disappear. In a minute or so, she saw him smile at the tall blond bitch, smile and put a hand lightly on her waist. Quick tears sprang up, burning her eyelids, and she had to close her eyes for a moment. Which was just as well, because Coco didn't *want* to see the growing interest on Leroy's face as the beautiful dancer tossed her long straight hair over one shoulder. Leroy had never favored a white girl before, but now it definitely appeared to be his favorite color.

"No, no, no!" yelled Shorofsky, throwing down his baton and glaring at Bruno. "You must hold a bow like this!" The old man arched his wrist. "Not like that!" He pointed to Bruno's right hand. "It's not your dick you're holding or a baseball bat. It's a violin bow, hold it with respect. Like . . ."

"Your dick," said Bruno, slyly.

The class giggled, and Shorofsky pushed his glasses up his nose in exasperation. It was so frustrating sometimes! Here was a boy with great abilities and no respect at all for serious music; it was criminal! He was murdering Mozart.

"Mozart wouldn't do this today," said Bruno suddenly.

"Do what?"

"This bowing business. He'd just plug his keyboard into a socket, play with his oscillators and have string quartets coming out of his fingers. And symphonies," he added, his eyes shining with his private vision.

The old man scowled. "And who would play these science-fiction symphonies?" he demanded.

"He would," replied Bruno confidently.

"All by himself?" Shorofsky's brow was darkening, a sure warning sign which Bruno chose to ignore.

"He'd overdub and mix. Of course, he wouldn't make the same old noise, exactly."

The old man's voice was like the rumbling of a live volcano.

"Noise?" he growled incredulously. "Mozart, noise?"

But Bruno was caught up in his dream. "He'd sound electric. He'd have spacier strings and horns and . . ."

"One man is not an orchestra," snapped Shorofsky, his face turning dark red.

Bruno shrugged. "Who needs orchestras? You can do it all with one instrument, a computer, and enough power." He looked around the little rehearsal hall with a grin. "You'd need more outlets."

"All by yourself?"

Bruno's smile was angelic. "You don't need anybody else!" he declared.

Shorofsky pounced. "That's not music, Martelli," he announced gleefully. "That's masturbation!" He picked up his baton again and waited for the waves of laughter to drown Bruno. When he saw the boy's face go scarlet, saw him sink into his seat, he chuckled with satisfaction and tapped on the little podium. Mozart, noise!

"Last year, we concentrated on simple observation," said Mr. Farrell. He looked around at his sophomore drama students. "This year we'll turn that observation inward and work on re-creating emotional states. Joy, sorrow, fear, anger. It'll be harder because you'll have to expose a little more of yourself."

Ralph Garcy whipped open his raincoat and "exposed himself" to Doris Finsecker. This time she laughed before she turned away. He was such a clown, always running a number on her. Sometimes he really *was* funny. She put him out of her mind and paid close attention to what Mr. Farrell was saying.

"For your first acting exercise this year, I want you to re-create a difficult memory, a painful moment. A time when you first realized something about yourself."

Doris glanced at Montgomery, and saw his brows come together in an anxious frown. What was wrong? Over the summer, they had drawn closer together than ever. With academic pressures abated, Montgomery and Doris had spent most of the summer indoors, either at the theatre or one of New York's many wonderful old movie houses, or reading plays up at Montgomery's apartment. Their friendship was cemented on the evening they had watched *Children of Paradise* together. Doris was seeing it for the first time, and Montgomery for the fifth. Holding hands, they looked on breathlessly as the classic drama of nineteenth-century French theatre unfolded on the screen: the loves and anguish of the players, the comedians and the tragedians, and the doomed love affair of the sensitive Baptiste and the enigmatic and glamorous Garance. Never, never had Doris seen theatrical life so convincingly portrayed; for the rest of the summer she would think about the film, and wonder if she could make a living as a mime, her face painted white like Baptiste's. Barrault was so wonderful; he could suggest any emotion with a flutter of his hand, a tiny movement of his mouth, a twist of his body, with no word uttered.

When they'd come out of the Carnegie Hall Cinema on 7th Avenue, they had discovered without surprise each other's tears, and as they walked hand in hand to the restaurant, Doris felt that their thoughts were united. She was certain that, no matter where their separate paths might lead, she and Montgomery would be friends forever.

Now, as the bell rang, and she gathered up her notebook and her Stanislavski, Doris mulled over Mr. Farrell's assignment. A painful memory. Where was she going to get a painful memory to re-create? A life as undramatic as hers . . . She'd have to talk to Montgomery. He'd know what to do.

Montgomery was waiting for her at their locker. Today was "blind Tuesday," and they'd both brought their lunch. "Blind Tuesday" was something Montgomery had made up, an exercise for them to practice. He thought it would be valuable for them to pretend that they couldn't see, to actually feel what it was like to be blind. To sharpen their senses of hearing and touch. They would take turns, and Doris would go first, so Montgomery could observe the effect and make corrections and comments.

At the locker, they got Doris ready. First, a pair of dark glasses. Then a cane with a white tip that Montgomery had signed out of the property room. This year, the Annie Hall look had swept P.A., and all the girls of fashion were wearing pieces of men's clothing begged, borrowed or swiped from fathers and brothers. Doris had managed to sneak one of her father's old vests from his closet, stuffing it into her bookbag so her mother wouldn't catch her. The vest was the requisite four sizes too large and, with the cane and the glasses, it gave Doris an authentically pathetic look. With Montgomery holding her by the arm, and her tin cup and lunchbag in her free hand, she tap-tap-tapped her cane slowly down 46th Street, attempting to feel what she couldn't see.

But the assignment was uppermost in her mind. "I can't find a painful memory," she told Montgomery. "I know I have them; I mean, my pain's as good as anybody else's."

"I have lots of them," said Montgomery, his humor tinged with bitterness. "You can borrow one of mine."

Doris negotiated her way at a snail's pace through a patch of junkies on Broadway. "How'm I doing?" she asked.

"Fine. I used to wet my bed. You can have that memory. That was painful."

Doris made a disgusted face. "No, thank you."

"Then there was the last time my father packed his bags and left us, or the first time my mother took the red-eye to Los Angeles and didn't come back for six weeks."

Doris felt his hand tighten on her arm, and heard the pain in his words. It's true, she thought, when you can't see your other senses are sharper. She knew Montgomery was lonely, but she had never realized until now *how* lonely.

". . . Or the first time I fell in love," said Montgomery in a curiously flat voice. He stopped suddenly, causing Doris to bump into him. A passing woman flashed Doris a look of sympathy and dropped a quarter into her cup.

Doris raised her glasses to look at the coin, then at Montgomery's face. There was such a look of suffering there that she felt her breath catch in her chest.

"Do you want to talk about it?" she asked in a small voice.

"Sure. Let's eat." He gave her a faint smile, and they crossed the street to George M. Cohan's statue, where they usually took their lunches on sunny days. There, as Doris chewed slowly on a sandwich that had lost all flavor, Montgomery told her about his most painful memory.

Why am I not more surprised? she asked herself. I guess that, deep inside somewhere, I must always have known. Doris looked around her. The world was still the same. The sky was blue, undercast with a reddish-brown pall of New York City pollution. Up the street, people were already in line at the discount theatre booth, which offered unsold tickets at half price before every performance. Nothing had changed. Montgomery was still Montgomery. She put the sandwich down in her lap.

"You're going to tell everybody that?" she asked softly.

Montgomery nodded. He looked directly into her eyes.

"It's the most painful memory I can think of," he told her.

Doris bit her lip. "He didn't say 'the most painful.' He just said 'painful.'"

"We're supposed to expose ourselves," Montgomery pointed out softly.

Doris shook her head. "Imagine what somebody like Ralph Garcy would say," she protested.

Montgomery's face broke into a smile. "A pie in the face comes with the job. That's what my mom says and she should know."

But Doris was still intent on keeping Montgomery from exposing himself to fresh hurts. "I don't get it," she said stubbornly.

A look of intensity came over the boy's narrow face, lighting his deep eyes. "A real artist must never be afraid of what people are going to say about him. Anyway, it was a moment when I realized something about myself."

"Maybe you didn't realize it right." She returned Montgomery's quizzical look. "I mean, everybody falls in love with their analyst. There's a word for that, isn't there?"

Montgomery nodded. "Homosexual," he said quietly.

When the first blast of music hit him, Bruno stopped in his tracks. "That's my music!" He gasped. "Some son of a bitch stole my tapes." Then he was galvanized into action. He tore out of the rehearsal room and down the stairs. The music, loud enough to be deafening, was coming from the street. The street? What the hell? He pushed his way through the mob of students pouring out the front door and tumbled down the steps of the school. He couldn't believe his eyes.

Angelo Martelli had drive his cab up to the front of the school and parked it smack in the middle of the street, blocking all traffic heading east. On the top of the Checker, he'd rigged a couple of public address speakers, powerful mothers, and from these speakers was pouring Bruno's music, loud enough to wake the dead in Trinity Churchyard sixty blocks downtown. Behind the cab, cars and trucks were shrieking angrily as fists pounded on horns. Drivers were cursing and yelling for Angelo to move that #$*&%#$ cab before I come over there and rip your face out, you #$*&(%%¢&#!!!

Boys and girls were running from all directions to the sound of the music, yelling with joy. Beaming, Angelo leaned proudly against his cab. "It's my son's music," he kept shouting. "My son *Bruno! Bruno Martelli!* He wrote the music. Today, Forty-sixth Street. Tomorrow, Madison Square Garden!" He waved cheerfully at the honking, cursing drivers hopelessly snarled in the traffic tie-up he'd created.

Bruno stood aghast, watching the incredible scene in front of him. They were dancing now, the boys and girls were dancing in the street, leaping and whirling and spinning around, singly and in couples and in groups, clapping their hands and snapping their fingers in time to the music. They didn't care that this was a public thoroughfare; they didn't care that it was in the middle of a busy working day, they cared only about the music. The dynamic rock and roll beat had lifted them and made them high, and now they were dancing as though nothing else was happening anywhere in the world.

"Sounds good," said Coco, arriving at Bruno's elbow. She gave him a grin and joined the dancers, spinning around on her thin legs as her own voice blared from the speakers, proclaiming that she would live forever. Fame was her name. In response to this message, even the staid music students were gettin' down and jiving. More and more youngsters were pouring into the street, lured by the joyous music. The school must surely be empty now.

The driver of the truck that was stuck behind Angelo's cab was purple with fury. "Move your stinkin' parade, will ya?" he shrieked, slamming on the horn again and again. "Whaddya think this is, Fifth Avenue?"

"What's the matter with you?" Angelo yelled back at him. "You don't like music?"

Still dazed, Bruno moved slowly to his father's side. "Papa, you should have left my tapes alone. They're not ready," he said shyly.

Angelo clapped his son proudly on the back. "Take a look at the people," he roared. "They don't know it's not ready. They like it!" He ran to his dashboard and turned up the volume on the speakers. The sound bounced off the stone buildings and ricocheted back into the street, sending the dancers into a wilder frenzy of movement. They were everywhere, weaving around the trucks and stalled cars, spilling over the sidewalks, treating 46th Street as though it were one big block party.

Which, realized Bruno with a sudden stab of pleasure, it was. They liked it. They were dancing to his music, *his*. It was *his* party. Maybe his father had thrown it, but the party was his. Bruno Martelli's. He began to smile.

He never stopped smiling, even when the infuriated truck driver, enraged beyond endurance, had thrown a punch at his old man, and the fighting started. He watched with a smile on his face, even when the other drivers ran out to join in the melee. The slugfest escalated into a full-scale brawl, but Bruno kept right on smiling.

Why shouldn't he smile? After all, even with a fistfight going on, the kids were still dancing.

2

THREE weeks after he'd given them the assignment, Mr. Farrell announced that he would begin to hear their recitations. He posted a schedule; Montgomery would be heard on the first day, Doris and Ralph on the last. During those three weeks, Doris had thought many times of begging Montgomery to give up his plan but every time she opened her mouth to speak to him, the words died on her lips. She honored his courage and his self-awareness; she was even a little envious of them, but she suffered for his pain, and for the hurt and rejection he would surely receive.

Yet, when the day came, and Montgomery sat up there on the stage, on a bare wooden chair, alone and speaking softly, Doris found that it was not nearly as bad as she had feared. There was silence as he spoke, and a few scattered embarrassed coughs greeted his "confession," but there was no one in the room who didn't take him seriously. Doris wasn't sure why she'd ever thought it would be different.

Montgomery spoke without apparent emotion. He didn't whine, or make verbal plays for pity. He related his story in a quiet, level voice that projected to the back of the little auditorium, yet everyone sensed the heavy burden of his words and felt some of the pain he merely hinted at.

It was a simple story, not unique. A lonely child, a famous mother who spent most of her time away, leaving a little boy in the company of strangers. A father who'd rejected him. His only friend, a handsome psychiatrist, helpful, caring. At first, the love he'd felt for this man had been the love of a boy for the father he'd never had. Later, new and confusing feelings had come to him. He was too young, at ten, to know what he was really feeling, but he did understand that children didn't feel quite that way about their parents, even their substitute parents.

"I thought I was just going through a stage," he said, shifting slightly in his chair. "That's what everyone told me, and it never worried me much when I was ten. Except they told me the same thing at twelve and fourteen. So, finally, my analyst leveled with me. He said it was probably a 'life choice.'" He stopped for a moment, as he always did when he thought of the word "choice." As though he'd *chosen* never to marry, never to have children of his own . . .

"Funny," he went on. "'Gay' used to mean such a happy kind of word once. Not that it bothers me. I'm pretty well adjusted, really. I mean, never being happy isn't the same as being unhappy, is it? Dr. Golden explains everything real well. I've had a lot of help . . ." He broke off, uncertain what to say next, how to end this. Silence greeted him from all parts of the auditorium.

After a moment, Mr. Farrell said, "Thank you, Montgomery." He paused. "Now, who's next?"

It was simple, after all. But Doris had a thought that she angrily dismissed as unworthy . . . yet, it did keep sneaking back in, like a nagging toothache. Would the kids in school look down on Montgomery, and would they look down on her, too, because they spent so much time together? It had been different last year, when everybody thought they were going together. Now that everybody knew . . . would she appear foolish? She smiled at Montgomery when he sat down next to her, and squeezed his hand to say that everything had gone off all right. His hand was as cold as ice, and the fingers were trembling.

My God, thought Doris suddenly. What an actor he is! He appeared to be so calm up there, so unemotional and rational, and all the time he was scared half to death! Her admiration for him, already profound, deepened.

When the bell rang, they stood up together and walked slowly out of the auditorium. As they passed the others, some of the boys and girls came forward to smile and say something friendly, while others averted their eyes, plainly embarrassed. Some of them had never known a gay person before. Never mind; they would learn to handle it. It might take time, but they'd come to realize that Montgomery was the same person he always had been, no more and no less. Those who had liked him would go on liking him.

137

The others, well, he was indifferent to them, too. Nobody is accepted and liked by *everybody*. If you ever meet anybody who is universally loved, don't trust him. He's keeping his true self hidden.

Just before lunch came makeup class. Doris loved it. They got to experiment with cosmetics and learn how to change their appearances to fit their roles. Montgomery was particularly adept at makeup, because his mother had taught him many stage tricks early in life, and he was showing Doris how to go from a baby to an old woman with a few strokes of a pencil and some Stagelight pancake. The makeup room was so small that only fifteen drama students were allowed in it at any time. There were only a few dressing tables, and many of the light bulbs had burned out and had never been replaced. Many of the boxes of cosmetics were battered and worn, and most of the jars were half empty; nevertheless, they were treated with reverence. At the back of the room was costume storage. Racks and racks of spangles, glitter, velvets, rags, imitation fur, paste jewels for a duchess, a dusty poet's cloak, a nun's habit—all waiting hopefully for their turn to shine in one more production.

Doris marveled as her sweet young face disappeared under a net of wrinkles created by Montgomery's deft pencil. She was so engrossed in her transformation that she didn't hear a hissing noise coming from behind the racks of costumes.

"Psst. *Psssttt!*"

Montgomery turned to look and, as he did so, the "curtain" of clothing was pulled aside, and out pranced an extraordinary creature.

Black garter belt holding up black stockings, pearl necklace clasped around a skinny adam's apple, a laced-up merry widow strapless bra, outrageously false eyelashes—it was Ralph Garcy. Head to toe he was dressed as Frank-N-Furter, the Transylvanian transexual transvestite Mad Scientist from *The Rocky Horror Picture Show*. Ralph, in full drag, minus the wig, was camping and swishing and making outrageously "feminine" faces.

"I thuppothe a fuck ith out of the quethtion," he lisped at Montgomery, batting his eyelashes furiously.

Doris drew her breath in angrily, but Montgomery just smiled, genuinely amused. Ralph could be very funny sometimes.

"Did you get the Valium?" demanded Ralph in normal tones.

Montgomery shook his curly head. "I had to change my appointment. I have a date. Dinner and *The Rocky Horror Picture Show*."

Ralph batted the eyelashes again. "Who's the lucky boy?" he cooed.

"I warned you this would happen," Doris told Montgomery. Her small hands were balled into fists and her chest heaved indignantly.

Ralph waved a deprecating hand. "Hey, that's just a joke, you know? Like, it just came out."

"Like me," smiled Montgomery.

"Yeah."

"I'm taking Doris," Montgomery said quietly.

Ralph gave him an expansive smile. "Look, it's your case. I don't care. Who gives a shit, you know?"

Montgomery shook his head. "It really doesn't matter." But, underneath, it mattered a great deal. Montgomery really liked Ralph, and he wanted his respect.

"Right, MacNeill," said Ralph, putting his hand on Montgomery's shoulder to show there were no hard feelings. "Ten milligrams when you can. I got bucks." He grinned over at Doris. "Hey, Doris, I was gonna tell you. I was reading through the trades today, and they've got an open call at the Diplomat . . ."

"Don't go to any cattle call," said a pretty black girl at the table near Doris. "They make you feel like shit."

But Ralph was poking around in his ridiculous drag, peering into his bodice as though for a slip of paper. "What did I do with it? They're looking for your type, Doris, you know. For a movie."

"This is a joke," said Doris suspiciously.

"No, I'm serious," protested Ralph. "They want an unknown young girl for something they'll be shooting in the city this summer. I thought of you right off. You'd be perfect for it."

Doris eyed him with mistrust. "What do you mean, 'perfect'?"

"Oh, you know. Kind of Jewish-paranoid." He kept patting at his costume, as though there were pockets in it. "I put it here somewhere . . ." he muttered.

"What's the name of this movie?" demanded Doris, her curiosity overcoming her suspicion.

"*I Was a Teenage Fag Hag,*" Ralph chortled gleefully.

She'd been had. With a yell, Doris jumped up and chased Ralph behind the rack of costumes. He cried out in exaggerated fear as she beat on his head, but he was laughing so hard that he soon surrendered, his

140

ribs aching. Somehow, unexpectedly, Doris found herself laughing, too. Sometimes Ralph was contagious.

All the way home, Doris planned what she'd wear to *Rocky Horror*. She'd been dying to go for months. She was the only girl she knew who hadn't seen it at least once. Most of the kids in the drama department were addicted to it, and they went back again and again, some of them as many as twelve or fifteen times. After all, how many movies give you the opportunity to dress up in costume and yell back at the screen? She'd heard so much about it; she could hardly wait.

The difficult part was going to be getting her mother's permission to stay out very late. The show didn't start until midnight, and with the shenanigans that came before it might be three o'clock in the morning before she got out of the Eighth Street Theater. Three o'clock in the morning in Greenwich Village with a boy on a Friday night. That would take some explaining to Mrs. Finsecker. Funny, thought Doris, Montgomery was so . . . safe . . . and yet she couldn't tell her mother that. She'd have to think of something else.

But when Doris reached home, she found her detested party dress washed and starched and laid out on her bed. Her mother was wearing a mud pack and had her hair up in rollers. Something was definitely in the wind.

What was in the wind was Jason Seth Silbermann's third birthday party. Mrs. Finsecker had "booked" Doris to sing.

"I *can't*, Mother!" Doris twisted her features into

what she hoped was convincing anguish. "I'm going to dinner with Montgomery, and then to the *theatre*. I can't disappoint Montgomery!"

"And I can't disappoint Mrs. Silbermann," said Mrs. Finsecker stolidly. "Your nice white blouse is ironed. You'll wear your pink dress with the ribbons. You look pretty in that."

"I *hate* my pink dress," moaned Doris.

Mrs. Finsecker took time out from tissuing off the mudpack to shrug. "So don't wear your pink dress." She was willing to concede a minor point, having obviously gained a major one.

"I'm not going, Mama!" protested Doris hopelessly.

Mrs. Finsecker knew better than to argue. "And gargle!" she ordered.

"I'm going out to dinner," she said, but she knew she was defeated.

"They'll have food at the Silbermanns'."

"It's not the food," Doris protested feebly, but Mrs. Finsecker overruled her with finality.

"It's an opportunity to perform," she told her. "Take advantage of it."

"But I promised Montgomery," murmured Doris sadly as she started to change clothes.

It was probably the worst moment of her life. Dressed like an overgrown Shirley Temple in the pink dress with the ribbons, Doris Finsecker sang "Happy Birthday to You" to a pampered, coddled three-year-old in a paper hat, who sat squirming and crying at the head of a table crowded with fourteen other three-year-olds, all making one horrible racket. Her brother Harvey thumped the piano in an out-of-tune accompaniment, and Mrs. Finsecker, proud of her talented daughter, kept getting in the way of the professional kiddie photographer as she snapped her inevitable Instamatic pictures of Doris to immortalize the occasion.

Barbra Streisand could never have gone through all this. This was humiliation . . . this was pain . . . this was . . . this was . . . this was her assignment for Mr. Farrell, that's what this was.

"Very good, Doris," said Mr. Farrell as she finished speaking. "And what did you realize about yourself?"

Doris took a minute to frame the answer. Finally, she looked out at the auditorium and said, "I don't like birthday parties. Or pink dresses. Or the Silbermanns. Or Brooklyn. Or even . . . being Jewish." She stopped to rephrase that. "I mean, it's not bad, but it's not *all* I am. I don't know who I am, but I never will if I just do what other people decide for me to do. I'm sixteen years old. I have to assert myself sometime . . ." She trailed off, a little embarrassed, but she noticed that Montgomery was smiling encouragement at her from the second row, and that several of the kids in the drama class were nodding their heads in agreement. She had reached them! She started to feel cleansed and new and energetic. She had reached them.

"Okay, Doris," said Mr. Farrell gently. "Ralph? You're next."

Mr. Farrell was worried about Ralph. Perhaps he'd been wrong to let him into Performing Arts. It wasn't that the boy lacked talent; no, he had a definite comic gift and an excellent sense of timing. But he was such a loner. In all the group exercises, only the surface part of him was present. Absent, buried inside, was an emotional core that remained untouched. Any attempt to elicit sensitive reactions had been met with wise-cracks, always wisecracks. He never let anybody get close to him, and he never seemed to trust anyone. An actor without trust . . . impossible. Farrell had known boys like Ralph before—boys who believed that feelings weren't manly, and that emotion left you open to the charge of being a faggot. Those boys usually didn't make it through Performing Arts.

This assignment was the test. Farrell gave it to every class, to separate those who could go on from those who couldn't. It was an assignment designed to free the actor from all self-restraints, to open his mind to his own possibilities. Every year, some of the kids took it as a joke, and prepared some cockamamie recitation because they couldn't or wouldn't face themselves. Others, like Montgomery, understood fully the importance of self-recognition to an actor. Even Doris had taken the first steps; now she was on the way. But Ralph? The most important thing he had yet to learn was that it wasn't enough to drop one-liners. A true comic actor was doing a harder job than a tragic actor, and he had to prepare for it even more thoroughly.

A painful moment in which you realized something about yourself. The revelation of a *real* emotion, not one copied from some late movie or "The Tonight Show." Ralph climbed the two steps to the stage more slowly than usual and sat himself down on the bentwood chair. He looked very small and thin and alone, nor did he look at Mr. Farrell or at anyone in the class. He began to talk.

"I come home from school, you know, like always. I'm late because I got one or two little pieces of business to attend to and it's January and Santa Claus has just ripped everybody off and split for Toy Town or Igloo City or somewhere. So, anyway, I find this note and it says my two chicks are in church and it's Thursday night, I think, and I wonder who died. That's a joke. That's supposed to be a joke," he said nervously. "And then I drop a little incense like always to relax and I switch on the TV and some dude is on talkin' about Freddie. Sayin' that Freddie Prinze put this gun in his mouth, makin' noise like he meant to kill himself. And everybody knows it was an accident."

Ralph sat silent for a moment, as though he were finished. But Mr. Farrell waited, drawn by the intensity of the boy's words and by the look of real grief on his face. Ralph turned in his chair to face his audience.

"He was jokin', you know. He was always jokin'. You had to laugh. He didn't even have to say anything, and sometimes you didn't even *want* to laugh. And you laughed anyway, you know. Like, it was a gift he had. All you had to do was look in that man's eyes to know he was not into death. The world wanted his ass 'cause he didn't think livin' was such a heavy trip and he was workin' its case real good. So they had to get him. Had to say he was *depressed and suicidal* . . ." Ralph's voice bore down on those words with bitter sarcasm ". . . 'cause the world gotta take itself real serious, you know. We can't have happy people walkin' around this planet. It doesn't pay."

Farrell was stunned to see tears spilling from the boy's eyes, but Ralph paid them no heed. He was totally caught up in this experience, reliving it there on the stage for everyone to see. He wasn't ashamed of these tears, nor of these feelings. For the first time, Farrell's doubts about Ralph's future began to dissolve.

"There's gotta be somethin' *wrong* with us . . . somethin' seriously wrong, so that the plastic surgeons and the witch doctors and the underarm deodorant people stay in business and we all gotta suffer and go to church and be sorry to the asshole God that fucked it up in the first place!"

He broke off, unable to continue. His entire body was contorted in rage and pain and he was glaring through his tears.

"Does all this make you realize something about yourself?" asked Farrell.

"What?" Ralph hadn't heard; he was still out there, somewhere, with the ghost of Freddie Prinze.

"How does it affect you?"

Ralph leaned back in his chair, wiping the tears off his cheeks with the back of one hand. "I'm here," he said bitterly. "In this school. Fuckin' it back. For Freddie."

The boy had locked himself right back into his shell. But that was all right. Mr. Farrell knew that, once the soul has been allowed to fly, nothing could keep it locked up for long. Having revealed himself today, Ralph would do so again, and that would begin

146

to free him to examine his own life, until he finally knew who he was.

"Take it easy, Ralph," said Mr. Farrell sympathetically. "You want them laughing *with* you, not at you."

Ralph stood up and looked down at his teacher. "I want 'em laughing, *period*."

The bell rang and the drama class began to disperse.

Doris pulled away from Montgomery's comforting arm and stood up. She was exhausted, first from her own efforts and then from Ralph's. Whew! As foreign as Ralph had always been to her, and as puzzling as his emotional entanglement with a dead comic was, she had understood his frustration on the stage, his anger and his impotence. How desperately he wanted to change what he couldn't change, and how powerless that left him feeling! Doris was no stranger to those feelings, and she had felt an unaccustomed empathy with that boy who was always all by himself. Something inside her spoke to him, impelling her to reach out to him and take his hand. But she couldn't bring herself to do it. She was too shy, and he would misunderstand and turn it into another of his dirty jokes. Besides, it was all too much for her. She'd already put in a full emotional day, and she was beat.

Mrs. Sherwood was perched on a ladder putting books away, when the swish of wheels caught her attention. Classes were changing, and in the corridor she could see throngs of boys and girls on the way to their next classes. Among them glided Leroy Johnson.

"Leroy!" she called.

The boy skidded to a halt. "Yes, ma'am."

"What are you wearing, Leroy?"

An innocent face met hers. A brown hand reached up and pulled something off a head. "A hat?" asked Leroy the cherub.

"On your *feet*, Leroy."

Leroy looked down in elaborate surprise and saw the roller skates attached to his high-top sneakers. He looked up again and presented another innocent smile. "Oh, those. Yeah, well, they helps me get around, so's I can fly from class to class quicker. Helps me get more learnin' in."

Mrs. Sherwood did not deign to answer such a load of blarney. "What about your book report?" she demanded.

"I done it."

"You *did* it."

"Yeah," agreed the boy. "One thousand words. I counted them."

"*The Best of Playboy* is not a *book* report."

"It's readin', ain't it?" Leroy's temper flared. Wouldn't the sour bitch ever let up? Didn't she realize what he'd gone through to get even this far? That woman never gave him an iota of credit.

"So is *1984*," snapped Mrs. Sherwood, scanning the titles on the shelves. "And *Huckleberry Finn* and *Great Expectations* and *Treasure Island*. You've heard of them?"

"I seen a couple of the movies."

"If you don't read, you're missing so much." She wished she could tell him that she *did* see the improvement in his work, the ferocity of his new efforts. But she wanted more, much more. Here was a boy with a brain who didn't know how to use it. The waste made her sick. No, it made her angry. She *would* get the best out of him, and she knew the only way she could reach him was to goad him. Soft words would earn only his contempt.

"I ain't into that stuff," said Leroy sullenly. "It ain't my jive."

Mrs. Sherwood ripped the volume of Shakespeare off the shelf. "Then try *Othello*," she instructed, tossing the book at him. "He's black. A thousand words in two weeks."

Angrily, Leroy caught the little volume and glared at it.

"Or what?" he demanded.

"Or you'll be skating right out of this school, Mr. Johnson."

Leroy took a long backward step to set the skates rolling, then glided away, scowling. He'd been having such a fine day, and now she'd spoiled it. Bitch! He turned to glare at Mrs. Sherwood, and when he saw she was no longer paying attention to him, he flipped her the royal bird.

Lisa pulled off her tights and stuffed them into her dance bag. She reached for her knee socks, but a hand touched her on the arm.

"Where are the blisters, Lisa?"

Lisa looked up. Miss Berg had come into the dressing room and was looking at Lisa's lily-white, pain-free feet.

"It's my shoes," said Lisa hurriedly. "They protect my feet."

"No shoe stops blisters."

"They're from Capezio," insisted Lisa.

"Get dressed and come into my office."

Miss Berg's office was a tiny cubicle plus an even tinier bathroom off the dance room, crowded with an oversize desk, a couple of wooden chairs and a file cabinet. A battered electric coffeepot was always plugged in, and the walls were covered with photographs of great dancers caught in mid-flight. Many of the photographs were signed personally to Miss Berg. Dance was Evelyn Berg's life. Since she had never married or had children, the dance students she placed every year with the major companies became substitute sons and daughters to her. There was no room among them for anybody less than excellent.

"I've been sick," was Lisa's first excuse as she sat in one of the wooden chairs.

"Dancers don't get sick. You're not working hard enough, Lisa."

"The doctor told me to take it easy for a week or two, until I feel okay."

Miss Berg raised one jet eyebrow. "Oh, so now it's the doctor's fault?"

"Don't you believe me? I brought a note."

Miss Berg sighed. There seemed no way to break through to this girl, to get her to understand that life was a very serious business indeed. Nothing worth achieving could be gained without toil and pain. "I believe you, Lisa. But I don't think I have room for you in this class anymore."

"But I brought a doctor's note!" In all the years

she'd gone to school, Lisa had learned that the doctor's note was sacred, never to be disputed; it was the excuse for everything from a missing homework paper to a skipped midterm. She couldn't believe her ears. She stared at Miss Berg, practically in shock.

Miss Berg was shaking her head. "There are too many other girls who take dancing seriously to waste time and space on someone who isn't dedicated," she was saying.

"I *am* dedicated!" protested Lisa, her cheeks growing hot.

"I'm sorry, Lisa. I don't see it."

Lisa sat back in her chair, unable to comprehend what was happening. This was a threat, right? Well, she'd have to work harder. She would! She'd really put out the sweat for Miss Berg. "I couldn't do anything else," she said in a choked voice.

"You'll find something," Miss Berg said dryly. It was hard for her to summon up a whole lot of sympathy for a pampered princess like this one. A girl like Hilary Van Doren was perhaps a hundred times more spoiled, but Van Doren was a dedicated dancer, and she worked like hell. This one wanted everything to come as a gift.

"I got into the school, didn't I?"

"We made a mistake. Sometimes it doesn't work out. I'm sorry." There was no mistaking her meaning.

"I don't know what I'll do if I can't dance." Lisa had risen to her feet.

"You'll get over it." Miss Berg moved swiftly to the door and made to open it. The interview appeared to be at an end.

"I'll work harder!" Lisa burst out.

151

Sympathy was beginning to awaken in Miss Berg's breast. And she couldn't let that happen; it interfered with the rational process of her judgment. "Maybe," was all she said.

"I promise! I'll be better!" pleaded Lisa, tears stinging her eyes.

Miss Berg shook her head again. "Better isn't good enough." She didn't want to be unkind, but it was the best thing for the girl to lose the phony illusions she carried with her. "I don't think you'll ever be good enough, Lisa. You don't have it. That's a hard thing to hear, and it's not a pleasant thing to say. But it's the truth and I'm saving you a lot of time and pain by saying it now."

"But I don't want to be the best," wailed Lisa.

That's just the trouble, thought Miss Berg. You have to want to be the best, want it more than anything else in the world. She sighed, "You won't be."

"I just want to be a dancer!"

"Well, you'll never be a Makarova, Lisa. We both know that. But you couldn't even get into the last row of the chorus of any show in town."

The girl was sobbing openly now. "I can't fail, Miss Berg. I only ever wanted . . . wanted . . . to be a dancer . . . What do I . . . tell . . . my mother?"

Miss Berg led her gently to the door, opened it and eased her out. "You'll get over it. Ask her to give me a call. I'll explain." She shut the door and leaned back against it. She was trembling; this scene had taken a lot out of her. But I'm glad it's over; it was a long time in coming. She'll get over it.

Miss Berg went into her pocket-sized bathroom to

wash her hands. The girl's sobs still echoed in her ears.

Lisa stumbled out of Miss Berg's office, not knowing where to go. Obviously not to her next dance class; all that was over now. Yet she was ashamed and afraid to go straight home, and certainly not in this distraught state. So she went to that place of comfort where generations of girls have sought refuge—the bathroom. There, she allowed herself the luxury of a breakdown, in full view of a sympathetic audience. The thing about kids is, it doesn't matter whether they like you or not. When a teacher picks on you, they close ranks around you, and temporarily you become one of them, a sister. So Lisa wailed and sobbed, and the other girls washed her face and patted her shoulders and reassured her that she was a good dancer and Miss Berg was just a mean old bitch. It made Lisa feel better, at least for the moment.

Coco Hernandez ordinarily had little use for Lisa Monroe. She knew the girl was a spoiled brat, and also she had troubles of her own. For one thing, Leroy was sending out some pretty heavy vibes to that Hilary number, and Coco did not take to that honkie messing with her man. In the second place, Bruno seemed to be getting to like her too much. Not that he ever actually came on to her. No, that wasn't his way. He was too shy for that. But Coco could feel his eyes on her, those big, sad, blue eyes. He watched her all the time—when they rehearsed together, when they mapped out new bookings for the band, even when they performed. Every time she looked at him, his eyes were eating her up. She waited in dread for him to say something to her. She liked him a lot; he was really a fine musician and a swell person. But she didn't want to get it on with him.

It wasn't only that she didn't go out with white boys. Bruno was certainly out of the common run of white boys. And it wasn't only that she was dating Leroy, which she was, or that she was basically a one-man woman, which she was. No, it was more like this: Bruno had so much buried inside him, aching to come out, that to start up with him would be like unleashing a tornado. *Heavy,* man! And Coco wasn't into very heavy relationships; she dreamed only of fame.

Yet, even with troubles of her own, and even though she didn't care a nickel's worth for Lisa, Coco discovered she had a little vein of sympathy for the girl. Jesus, imagine if *she* had no talent and got thrown out of dance! Brrrrr. So she rummaged around in her big denim tote for Kleenex, and she told the sobbing Lisa that everything was gonna be okay. For the rest of the day, Lisa hung out with Coco, pathetically grateful. Even after school, when the kids decided to head for Chinatown to get some black bean spareribs, Lisa tagged along with them.

By now, she had stopped crying, but the dark wings of depression had folded around her. Tagging after Coco and her friends, she had no idea what would become of her. After all the money that her family had invested in her dance lessons, how could she face them? What could she tell them? She had let them down. They'd be so disappointed in her; they'd had such high hopes. Here they'd been thinking that their precious daughter was the best, when all along she'd been the worst. Yes, the worst. She admitted it now.

The downtown platform of the IRT 50th Street Station was almost deserted at this time of day. An hour or so later, when rush hour began, it would be jammed with hundreds of impatient commuters going home from work. But now there were only the kids from Performing Arts and a handful of tired New Yorkers with closed faces.

It was a dingy platform, in desperate need of repair, its walls covered with graffiti. In the exact middle of it was a large puddle of brackish water. As soon as Coco saw the puddle, she turned into Gene Kelly in *Singin' in the Rain*. God, she loved that movie, especially the famous scene where Gene, in love with Debbie Reynolds, sings and dances in a rainstorm, splashing through the puddles joyfully, blissfully unaware that he's soaked to the bone. Coco had seen the film maybe a dozen times. Recently, they'd played it at Radio City, and Coco saw it for the first time on a huge screen with real good sound. It was a knockout, and she never grew tired of it.

Now she broke into the song, grinning and mugging, and began to tap in the puddle of water, doing the steps she'd picked up from Kelly in the movie. "SSSiiiiiingin' in the rain, just singin' in the rain," she belted out, in a voice surprisingly big for so little a girl. Her sneakered feet moved intricately through the water, soundlessly tapping. Delighted, all the girls crowded around her to watch. All of them but Lisa, who sat forlorn on the splintery wooden station bench.

"I'm laughin' at clouds," trilled Coco. She was never so happy as when she was performing. She loved to sing, to dance and to act, and when she could put them all together, as she was doing now, she was in her element. Now that she had an audience, she sang even louder and danced even faster.

From down the long, dark subway tunnel she could hear the train coming. If it was an express, it wouldn't stop, but go hurtling past them with a rackety explosion of sound and disappear into the tunnel farther down. If it was a local, it would stop and carry them down to Chinatown. She'd better sing faster. That old train would be here any minute.

"I'll waaaaalk down the lane." The girls were clapping their hands, beating time for her. Out of the corner of her eye she saw Lisa stand up and walk toward them. Good, maybe she'd lighten up a little, it was like carrying Bad Vibes Failure around with them. Coco tried the tricky step of one-foot-on-the-curb-and-one-in-the-gutter, but without a curb or a gutter, it didn't come off. Lisa passed the group and headed toward the platform's edge. The train was speeding toward the station now and Lisa was dangerously close to the tracks.

Jesus! What the hell was she doing? You could get killed that way! Coco broke off her song and started forward, but it was too late. With a deafening roar, the train rushed by them at seventy miles an hour, not stopping. At the last minute, Coco saw something hurtling through the air, into the path of the train. She screamed, a heart-freezing scream, and she closed her eyes in terror.

The train passed. Coco opened one eye and dared to look down at the tracks. Lying there, spread out and mangled, almost past recognition, were Lisa's toe shoes. And her leotards. And her dance bag.

As for Lisa herself, she was looking down at her

discarded dance bag and shrugging her shoulders. "Screw it," she said lightly to Coco. "If I can't dance I'll switch to the drama department."

Coco blew out her breath in relief tinged with annoyance. "You might as well," she told Lisa in disgust. "You sure are one hell of an actress!!"

"I heard the bitch came down real hard on her," said Phenicia to Coco in dance class the next day.

Coco shrugged. "So? Life comes down hard."

"She took it real bad, the dumb kid," said Leroy, who was dancing nearby.

Coco decided not to tell them about Lisa's change of attitude. It was nobody's business but her own. "Better she realizes it now than OD-ing in some motel room at thirty."

"I think you might show a little more sympathy, dear," drawled Hilary Van Doren, with a flick of her eyes toward Leroy.

"Change partners," called out Miss Berg, and Coco found herself dancing across from Hilary.

"I'm not 'dear,'" she snapped.

Hilary put on a smile of amusement. *"Evidemment,"* she agreed. "You're not *très* sensitive, either."

That bitch and her goddamn French. "I'm a professional," replied Coco coldly. "A few unkind words aren't gonna wipe me out. I know it's not gonna be all standing ovations."

"Certainly not for you, my dear," purred the blond princess.

Coco's temper snapped. "Look, I'm not 'my dear,' " she exploded. "You can fuck 'my dear'!"

Hilary gave Leroy a dazzling smile, which he returned. "Well, thank you," she said. "That might be fun." Her expression said she wanted to jump on Leroy's bones.

"That might be impossible," retorted Coco. "Leroy ain't into vanilla."

"It might be a welcome change from black cherry," said Hilary scornfully.

" 'The darker the berry, the sweeter the juice,' honey."

"Yes, but who wants diabetes?"

"Change partners," called Miss Berg once more, and Hilary slid gracefully over to Leroy, who was just eating up all the attention. There wasn't anything in the world he dug more than to see two fine foxes fighting over his bod. It made him feel two times a man. And the blonde was prime. Oooooooeeeee, she had a sweet fine head of hair. And those legs! Gonna get me some o' that, he told himself. And soon.

Coco wasn't blind. She had seen this coming, and now it appeared to have arrived. But what could she do about it? She believed in freedom. Wouldn't it be two-faced to tell Leroy whom he could and couldn't see? Anyway, it would be damn near impossible. She really couldn't picture Leroy taking hassle from a chick. One word, and he'd fly out the window so fast she'd never see him again. Shit! The only thing to do was keep her mouth shut and hope that miserable Hilary Van Doren breaks one of her legs. Better yet, both.

If it weren't for English class, Leroy would have been on top of the world. Everything was going so fine. Thanks to Coco, he was doing pretty well in Spanish class. Math was not difficult. In history, he borrowed notes and homework, and physics class had even become a stone gas sometimes, with those cornball experiments. English, man, that was the big hassle.

But Leroy brightened. Here he was, getting an education, something he'd never thought he needed or would have, and that was the price he had to pay to dance. And dance class was the best, man, the finest of the fine. He'd gotten used to Miss Berg, and she to him, and after he'd worn tights a couple of times, he'd even gotten used to *them*. They no longer bothered him, and he wore them un-self-consciously. He was wearing them now, as he walked along the street toward his house.

He was thinking about Coco and Hilary, and feelin' real good. Two fine chicks, and they both wanted him. And the best part was, he didn't have to choose. He could have them both. If that made Coco unhappy, it was just too bad. He needed a change of pace. Not that he was serious about either one of them, but it gave his ego a boost that Hilary had put the moves on him. She was probably the best-looking thing in the school. He'd never had a white girl before, but Hilary was making it very plain that she knew what she wanted, and what she wanted was Leroy Johnson.

He turned the corner, and chuckled as he saw the decorated Trans-Am convertible coming toward him. He hadn't seen those dudes in weeks, and they used to hang out together all the time. The fact was, he didn't have that much time for friends anymore, what with the long school hours and the heavy homework schedule, not to mention Hilary and Coco. But he was glad to see them now, maybe they could go for a pizza or some fried chicken. He was suddenly starving. He raised one arm to wave at the convertible, and it made a U-turn and drove up to the curbside.

"Hey, faggot!"

Who were they talking to?

"Hey, faggot, pussy faggot, watchoo doin' up here in a man's neighborhood?" They were catcalling to him, making obscene gestures, pointing to his tights and his books.

Leroy froze in horror. *Him,* they were talking to him, calling him names, mocking him. He opened his mouth to protest, but rage overtook him. Faggot! He'd show them faggot. He'd shove faggot up their noses! He looked around him and spied a garbage can. Instantly he seized it and raised it high over his head. Running to the car, he dumped the contents of the garbage can—rancid food, ashes, papers—on the heads of the surprised boys. Then he hurled the can through the windshield, picked up his books and ran like lightning for home.

Toward the end of the school year, Bruno had prevailed upon Mr. Shorofsky to allow him to conduct an electrified concert. Against his better judgment, Shorofsky had given in, but now he watched in horrified distaste as Bruno amplified the violins, the horns and even the reeds. Miles of heavy electrical cable lay coiled on the stage, a menace to life and limb. Extension cords, their mother-sockets crammed with plugs, led from every instrument to the outlets. If this was the future of music, Shorofsky was glad he was too old to be around for much of it.

Bruno hummed contentedly as he made his connections. He was really digging this. In the last few weeks, orchestra rehearsals had become fun, not hassle. Working with his fellow musicians, listening to them play his special arrangements had given Bruno a new kind of pleasure. For years he'd been down in the basement all by himself, locked away from the real world in his own private world. Coco had helped him out of the basement, Coco and the band. Now, working with a real orchestra, Bruno had begun to realize that Mr. Shorofsky was right—music was more than an isolated, private pleasure. It could be an experience of sharing. And Bruno was going to share his music with Shorofsky—right now.

The wiring completed, Bruno mounted the podium with a happy smile. He raised his baton; the musicians picked up their instruments. He brought the baton down. With a loud sizzle, the auditorium was plunged into darkness. The fifth floor was plunged into darkness, as was the third and the second, and the fourth and the first. Bruno had blown all the fuses; the

161

fuse box had melted; the school would have to be re-wired.

As chaos descended, a fitting chaos for the end of a school year, Mr. Shorofsky managed a bitter smile. Maybe the future wasn't quite ready yet for Bruno Martelli. He didn't know it, but he'd missed the sharing. It would have to wait for another time.

JUNIOR YEAR

1

RALPH Garcy came back to school determined to work. It had been a long, rotten summer, brutally hot, and his usual job, delivering groceries for the A&P, had not been the rainbow he'd been chasing. He had originally thought of himself as mounted like a prince on that bicycle cart, his big radio playing the top Spanish station while he dropped off the bags and collected the tips. Actually, it had turned out much different. You can't leave a radio unattended on the streets of the south Bronx, so the first day Ralph had dragged it up the stairs with every delivery.

The second day, and thereafter, he'd left his radio at home.

It had been miserable. Even if the customers lived in the projects, with elevators, the elevators were damn near always broken and Ralph had to take the stairs. But most of his customers lived in tiny, ratty, walk-up apartments, usually on the top floor. Because almost all the younger housewives took their bags home in shopping carts, Ralph was left with the aged and poor. Living on small Social Security checks or on welfare, how could they afford to give him a tip? Often they would apologize in trembling voices, anxious that he might get angry and beat them up. Ralph felt so sorry for some of them he'd almost been moved to give *them* money.

The bicycle cart had proven hard to manage, with all the potholes and broken sidewalks in the barrio. The damn sun beat down on his head without mercy. So, all summer long, it was the crummy streets and the heavy bundles and the sweltering apartments. All for $3.50 an hour and no tips! There had to be a way out.

Performing Arts was the way out, decided Ralph. He still dreamed of following in Freddie's Guccis, but he knew that he needed contacts and friends. Two years at P.A. had shown him that the school had powerful friends, and that they looked after their own. He needed them. He could use them.

And he had to admit to himself that he was enjoying his years there. It had never occurred to him in the past that he would ever enjoy school, or get anything out of it. But he was learning many valuable things. More than that, he was starting to make friends. He always made them laugh; they loved him for his constant stream of jokes. So, as he broiled and toiled, Ralph had found himself looking forward to the start of the school year.

As juniors, they would be required to perform

more. Every assembly brought its dance concert, or music recital, or dramatic reading. It was the upper-class students who provided the bulk of it, testing their skills in front of an enthusiastic but critical audience. This was what they had all been waiting for; it was why they had come to P.A. They had to perform.

When drama class reconvened and assignments were handed out, Montgomery chose to direct a scene from *Marty*, the touching old Paddy Cheyevsky story of a Bronx butcher and a lonely schoolteacher. Neither one of them beauties, they meet at a dance and find that each of them manages to ease the other's loneliness a little. And they shyly fall in love. It wasn't surprising that Montgomery chose a scene that dealt with loneliness. It wasn't surprising that he chose Doris Finsecker to play the part of the schoolteacher. But he surprised even himself by asking for Ralph Garcy to play Marty. Brash, self-confident Ralph to portray a shy and lonely middle-aged man! Curious, Mr. Farrell agreed.

They decided to rehearse the scene at Montgomery's place, one block up Broadway at 47th Street. Doris had been there a couple of times, but Ralph never. He couldn't believe it when Montgomery took him into the Palace Theatre building. Who the hell lives over a theatre? He hadn't even known there were apartments there.

When he saw Montgomery's place, Ralph's eyes bugged out of his head. It had once been a rehearsal studio, and the rooms were vast and empty. Oh, there was a chair here, and a little table there, but no sofas, no easy chairs, no TV, no nothing. *Nada*.

"Hey, turkey, what happened to the furniture? You get ripped off?"

Montgomery smiled. "It closed in Cincinnati."

"How's that?"

"My mother kept saying that she was going to fix it up when she got into a long run. But she's got a lousy choice in plays. Sorry."

"I think it's very nice," put in Doris defensively.

But Ralph was busy wandering around, marveling, opening doors, checking the place out. There was a tiny kitchen, little more than a kitchenette, its shelves holding boxes of crackers and canned soups, while all that was in the refrigerator was a couple of Cokes and a piece of American cheese. Montgomery had chosen the smallest room to be his bedroom, but it was still pretty big, and his single bed looked tiny up against one wall, with a little black-and-white TV at the foot.

Ralph had never seen so much living space before. And all of it belonged to only one person. *¡Ay, María!* Fifteen Puerto Rican families could fit in here, with all their furniture and TVs, and still have room to take in boarders. He shook his head at how crazy life was.

But what gassed him the most was the huge Palace Theatre sign, right outside Montgomery's front windows. With darkness falling the sign was beginning to bathe the room in pink neon light, turning it into a misty fairyland, the ghost of some dead amusement park. Wow! Imagine old M&M never telling anybody about this. If it were mine, I'd have parties every day. With loud music, yeah, and good grass and all the hottest ladies. But he was forgetting. Montgomery wasn't into ladies.

"It's perfect," Ralph said, spreading out his hands. "Okay, Mr. Director, what do we do?"

Montgomery smiled and handed out the playbooks. "Page one. From the top."

They worked for hours, then went out for an Orange Julius and a frank and came back to work some more. They were into it now, into the feel of the story and its underpinnings. A surprising chemistry was developing between Doris and Ralph. Disparate though their acting styles were in the beginning, under Montgomery's direction, and with their own growing familiarity with the lines and with their characters, their styles began to mesh, retaining a basic hint of the difference between a crude butcher and a schoolteacher. This was going to be good; Montgomery felt a glow of satisfaction.

It was lovely to work with friends. The three of them . . . it's as though we were meant to be friends, meant to be together, he thought. This was working, because the three of them were working on it. Odd, he'd been drawn to the script because of its emphasis on loneliness, but since the three of them had been working on it, he hadn't felt lonely at all.

They were concentrating on the dance scene, the scene in which the two lovers meet for the first time. Doris and Ralph had never done "touch dancing," so their awkwardness on the floor was natural and very convincing. Montgomery, holding a flashlight beam steady on a mirrored globe, was creating the colored lights effect of a cheap dance hall. The Palace sign provided an eerie glow that was now a deep orange-red. In each other's arms, Doris and Ralph moved in a slow circle as they spoke their lines.

" '. . . You get kicked around long enough you get to be a real professor of pain,' " Ralph was saying. " 'I know exactly how you feel. And I also want you to know I'm having a very good time with you now and really enjoying myself. So you see, you're not such a dog as you think you are . . .' "

Doris smiled up at him and said quietly, " 'I'm having a very good time, too.' "

" 'So there you are,' " said Ralph as Marty. " 'So I guess I'm not such a dog as I think I am.' "

" 'You're a very nice guy, and I don't know why some girl hasn't grabbed you off long ago.' "

" 'I don't know, either. I think I'm a very nice guy. I also think I'm a pretty smart guy in my own way.' "

" 'I think you are,' " said Doris shyly, still in character.

Montgomery nodded happily; there was a delicacy about this scene, a sweet tenuousness, that they had captured at last. He looked up from his playbook to find Doris and Ralph kissing, their arms wrapped around each other. That couldn't be right! Hurriedly, he flipped through the pages.

"You shouldn't kiss here," he called to them. "There's a whole speech yet . . ."

But the boy and girl, lost in a world of their own, kept on kissing. This wasn't playacting; this was for real.

Loneliness struck Montgomery a sudden ice-fisted blow to the heart. In one split second, they were no longer three. They were back to being two plus one, only this time he was the extra person, not Ralph. Suddenly, he felt like an intruder, even though the apartment was his. He rose to his feet. Doris and Ralph were still locked together in the same embrace. They had forgotten that Montgomery was in the room.

The glass on the second floor window announced Glades Studios in decorative capital letters. Underneath, in smaller printing: Rentals by the Day or Week. By the light of a street lamp, Leroy could barely make out the letters as he followed Hilary to the entrance. It was a seedy building like a hundred others in the Times Square area.

Inside was a long, narrow hallway lit by one sixty-watt bulb. It smelled of stale urine and of unwashed shopping bag ladies who took shelter there. The hallway led to a flight of concrete steps whose cracks were barely hidden by an ancient linoleum runner. OOOooeeeee, thought Leroy. This place does not deelight my eyes or my nose. With a shrug, he followed Hilary up the stairs. She didn't seem to notice the smell or the roaches that scuttled around the cracks in the linoleum.

On the second floor, Hilary put her hand into the pocket of her red fox jacket and took out a large key. Unlocking the studio door, she glanced back at Leroy with a small smile, making certain that her long, thick hair swung attractively over one shoulder with the movement of her neck. She snapped on the light.

It was a dance studio, pure and simple. A barn of a room, with the regulation barre at one end, facing a tall, broad mirror, where the dancers could see their movements. The floor was in good condition, and

171

there were a couple of straight-backed wooden chairs, the kind you see in old-fashioned offices everywhere. At the far end of the room was a mattress set on top of a box spring without legs, and covered with an Indian throw of cheap cotton. Behind a door was a tiny dressing room, where no more than two or three very slender dancers could change at one time. That and a water cooler were the last two features of the room.

Although some heat was hissing from a single radiator under the windows, the room was cold. But that was better for dancing. Leroy gave the place a final inspection and nodded his approval to Hilary, who smiled back.

Hilary disappeared into the dressing room for ten minutes. When she came out she was wearing a leotard and tights of a striking orchid color. The ribbons of her toe shoes were untied, and she moved carefully to the barre. She raised one long, slim, glorious leg, and bent toward it to tie her slipper. Out of the corner of her eye she could see Leroy watching her, and she knew that she made a striking picture, ankle on the barre, long hair falling forward, the sensuous arc of her slender back and arms.

Suddenly aware that he was staring at her, Leroy felt a rush of embarrassment, and he made for the tiny dressing room. As he stripped down to a T-shirt and cutoffs, he felt a strange pounding in his pulse points. He imagined he could actually feel the blood moving in his veins. He had never felt like this with any girl before, and there had been plenty of girls. He could barely put a name to his feelings, but there was a constriction in his chest that made breathing difficult. Hilary was so completely different from anybody he had ever known. Her aloof manner, her feeling of superiority, set her apart from the others. Yet, whenever she looked at him, her eyes were . . . not exactly warm, but promising. Promising, teasing . . . who the hell knew? Leroy felt insecure in her presence. It was a new feeling, and he didn't exactly like it. Sometimes he felt she was laughing at him.

A strain of eerie, slow music came in through the dressing room door. It was a melody that Leroy had never heard before, yet it sounded somehow familiar, music heard in a dream or an earlier life. He came out of the dressing room and into Hilary's world.

She was dancing. She had snapped off the overhead lights, and only the ghostly street light coming in through the windows illuminated her. The strange, slow music was coming from a cassette recorder, and the girl, lost in the circular space of the dance, was dipping, swaying and turning to its stately rhythms. In the semi-darkness, she appeared an alien creature from an undiscovered world, a world without speech, but only movement.

Leroy felt a lump rising in his throat. He had never seen anything so beautiful, so untouched, as this girl absorbed in her dancing. The slow music began to reach him, and suddenly, he, too felt its attraction. He moved silently onto the floor, and joined her in the dance.

They did not touch. They did not even dance near each other. All the same, they were as close as an embrace. Hilary moved in the classical patterns of the ballet, while Leroy found his feet and body creating steps and movements he'd never done before. Slow, sweeping, sensuous, he wove patterns around the light girl in the toe-shoes. The moth wasn't moving toward the flame. Instead, the flame flickered around the moth, threatening to consume her, yet never touching her flesh. Around them both, the formal patterns of the music—Ravel's *Pavane for a Dead Princess*—spread a melodic mantle.

There was a joy in this dancing that Leroy had never known before. The exhilaration of moving slow and free, like a creature whose home was the sea-bottom, sent the blood racing through his muscular young body. He could not define the look on Hilary's face as he perceived it in the haloed light, but he knew that her feelings matched his own. Exaltation and rapture.

The music grew more insistent, and Leroy's steps brought him closer and closer to Hilary. Suddenly, the girl bent forward like a blossom on a vine, and reached her long arms out to him. He danced to her side and embraced her, and she leaned her head against his shoulder in the dance. All at once, they were moving as one person, their steps neither classical nor modern, but a co-mingling of both. In the cold room, Leroy felt the warmth of Hilary's body spread to his, and his to hers. Passion, deep and demanding, began to rise in his blood.

He turned his face to hers, and their lips met in a kiss. Insistently, he began to move her toward the mattress in the corner. She allowed herself to be moved. Their lips still joined, they came to the bed as the music swept to its grand climax, and together they fell on it, kissing deeply, their hands urgent on each other's bodies.

Dressed only in a thin shirt and cut-off jeans, Leroy

was able to take his clothing off in a time no longer than the beat of a heart. Hilary's slippers, leotard and tights took longer, and he watched her slim body free itself until her nakedness matched his. He had never seen anything so beautiful, so fragile in appearance.

But Hilary wasn't fragile. She had the youthful strength of tensile steel, and her grasp was demanding, her passions urgent, matching Leroy's moment by moment until all the barriers of race and circumstance had broken down before their excitement and their ultimate release.

Afterward, they had almost nothing to say to each other. But the minutes of love-making lay between them, silent and shining and untouchable by anything that might happen later.

━━━━━━━━━━

They'd played a bar mitzvah at Shimkin Caterers in Brooklyn, and they'd been good, very good, even though the bar mitzvah boy had insisted on sitting in on drums for one of the sets. What the hell, Bruno had let him. The kid was terrible—worse than terrible—but the parents had loved it, the relatives had eaten it up and the photographer had snapped thirty-six exposures. Fifty bucks extra had come out of it as a tip from the proud father, and the banquet manager had promised them other gigs. They'd been a hit, especially when Coco, in a see-through blouse, had sung "Hava Nagila" for them. They thought it was adorable, this little *schwartze* singing Hebrew.

So why was he so depressed?

He knew why. It was Coco. He knew she'd been good for him, taking him out of himself, bringing him up from his basement, making him perform. He felt taller now and less shy. Everywhere he went pretty girls came on to him. He had money in his pocket, money that came from his own work, not his father's. Everything was going great. Everything except his relationship with Coco.

Relationship, that was a laugh! It was a business partnership, and she never let Bruno forget it. Oh, sure, she liked him, and she treated him well in an offhand way, like a dog that needed to be walked daily, fed and petted occasionally. But she never opened to him, never confided in him, so that seeing her every day had become for Bruno a crazy kind of torture.

He knew she was unhappy. He'd heard that Leroy Johnson was going out with Hilary Van Doren, if "going out" was the right phrase for what they were doing. He'd heard that Hilary had a place of her own, a dance studio she'd rented, and that Leroy and she "rehearsed" there evenings and nights. Leroy was still supposed to be seeing Coco, but take tonight, for instance. He'd promised to pick her up after the gig at Shimkin's and take her to a hot, new downtown place to dance. But did he show? No. And did he call? No. So now he and Angelo were taking Coco home in the cab.

Coco sat with her face pressed to the glass of the window, not saying anything, crying inside. Shit! Why didn't he phone her, instead of just standing her up? She'd been great tonight, the crowd had loved her, and it had given her a high like nothing else. And now she was down, way down. Moanin' the blues over some worthless guy. She felt like a junior-miss version of Billie Holiday, but even that thought couldn't make her smile.

Why doesn't she confide in me? thought Bruno. How many friends does she have? If only she'd open up and talk about it, maybe I could convince her to let me help her forget him. That creep! He doesn't deserve to have her . . . But what could you expect from a dancer? Their brains are in their feet.

He'd written her a song . . . well, maybe not only for her, but for himself, too. As independent as Coco seemed to be, she was still a child underneath. He'd tried to capture it in the song, "Out Here on My Own," when he wrote about vulnerability and self-doubt, about trying to fit in.

Last week he'd played it through for her once, letting her get the feeling of the melody. Then Coco had sat next to him on the piano bench, and had played and sung it through. It had given him such a charge, listening to her clear, sweet voice singing his music, his words, words about love and pain. He hardly dared to look at her while she was singing, but when she'd finished, their eyes met. He put his hand out to touch hers, but before he could, Coco, shaking her head, had said, "Sentimental shit!" Incredible! She was four or five people, all in the same little package. But she sure had talent.

Now Angelo was pulling up outside the address Coco had given him. It was a dignified and expensive doorman building on Central Park West, its stone facade interrupted by a canopied awning.

"You live here?" Angelo asked Coco.

Coco smiled briskly. "My sister lives here. I'm always welcome."

"Nice place," said Angelo. "Very fancy. I'll wait for you. Until you get inside. You never know."

Coco looked a little nervous. "No, it's okay," she said hastily. "It's a good neighborhood." She fumbled in her bag and brought out a handful of crumpled bills, offering them to Angelo. "Look, it's not much, but . . ."

Angelo interrupted with a wave of his hairy hand. "Please. It's not necessary. I should pay *you*. I play your tapes for my customers. They love that stuff. My tips go up twenty percent . . ."

Coco smiled and started to get out of the cab, but Angelo touched her hand to stop her.

". . . and my son is happy," he said softly, with a nod at Bruno, who sat back with his eyes closed, his face turned away.

Coco looked. Bruno certainly didn't *look* happy, but she knew what Angelo was driving at. She dreaded what was coming, and tried to avert it. "He's writing good shit, too. We're gonna be all over the charts one of these days, mark my words," she said quickly.

"*You* make him happy," Angelo told her. "You know that."

But Coco was not yet ready to acknowledge a relationship between them, especially not to Bruno's old man. "We're a hot team," she said lightly.

"You make him . . . hotter. You know what I mean."

Coco looked him straight in the eye. "Sure I know. I have that effect on people. What can I do?" She

178

waved goodbye and got out of the cab, ducking under the canopy of the apartment building as though she were going to enter. But she didn't enter. As soon as Angelo had driven off, Coco gave the doorman a weak grin, then hustled to the corner to grab the subway uptown. Central Park West. She should only live so long.

Bruno, looking back, saw Coco's maneuver, and it made him smile despite his depression. She had style, you had to admit it. She was a great little hustler, a sensational promoter. And she was a hot little singer and dancer. But when it came to taking care of herself, she had less on the ball than his cat Eleanor. When was she going to smarten up, give Leroy the heave-ho and settle down and let Bruno take care of her?

———————————

Hilary had been seeing Leroy for some time, long enough for her to know that she was in no hurry to let him go. There was something about him she couldn't put a name to, a kind of fire smoldering underneath his cool exterior. It thrilled her every time she saw him. He would be a great dancer someday, because he brought the same passion to his work that he did to his loving.

They'd been meeting mostly in her "studio." She knew the kids in the dance department were talking about them, but she didn't care. Their dancing was such an exciting experience. Hilary was trained in classical ballet, but what she and Leroy had put together was part classical, part jazz, unlike anything she'd ever seen on stage. It was one of the things that kept them from getting tired of each other. Neither of them pretended for a moment to be in love.

For months, Hilary had been wanting to bring Leroy home to the town house just west of Park Avenue where she lived with her father and stepmother. Meeting family wasn't Leroy's bag, so he kept turning Hilary down. But he had to admit that he was real curious about how rich white folks lived. Was it true they ate off gold plates and slept on silk sheets? Was there color TV in the bathroom? To all his teasing questions, Hilary gave the same teasing answer, come home with me and see.

Then, one day, she asked him if he was afraid to meet her father, and that did the trick. Leroy Johnson was not about to be afraid of anybody, never mind some middle-aged honkie with a gut made of blubber. So he told Hilary—casually, of course—that he'd be around to check out her place that evening.

They left together after school, taking a cab uptown, for which Hilary paid with a twenty-dollar bill pulled carelessly from a Vuitton billfold. When they stood on the sidewalk outside Hilary's home, Leroy realized that he'd never been on a street like this in all his seventeen years. It looked like a movie set, this row of four-story town houses with imitation gas-lamp fixtures and brightly polished brass knockers.

The front door of Hilary's house was painted green, and it bore a set of white numbers with long, curling tails. On either side of the door stood tightly clipped dwarf yew trees, and the windows featured green metal window boxes crowded with pink geraniums, white petunias and trailing ivy. For the first time, Leroy thought he might be making a mistake. But he squared his shoulders and followed Hilary inside.

He'd never been inside an elevator this small before. He had no idea that it was a private elevator, exclusively for the use of the Van Dorens. It was mirrored and gilded, and had a tiny bench covered in pink damask, so that ladies might sit. But Hilary wasn't into sitting, she was busy filling Leroy in on the family relationships.

"My mother was French," she told him enthusiastically. "And very beautiful. Straight out of some medieval chateau. And she danced. Every night. Hours and hours. Daddy was in Washington or Dallas or out to dinner with clients and my mother was with Tchaikovsky or Ravel . . . or Mantovani. I had funny little legs and fangs for teeth and thirty or forty too many pounds. I envied her shamelessly. But she said I was lucky. That I'd have a whole lifetime to spend creating something beautiful. 'Beautiful isn't something you're born,' she would say. 'It's something you practice.'"

Leroy was getting nervous from Hilary's chatter. It didn't occur to him that the chatter was a sign that Hilary was nervous too.

"You'll meet Claudia, my stepmother—trainee witch," babbled Hilary as they left the elevator and faced the door of the apartment. "And no cracks about being Chinese, she's had her eyes fixed. She recuperated in Palm Springs and had her purse stolen." She fumbled around in her large shoulder bag, finally emerging triumphant with a set of keys.

"She lost all her credit cards. Daddy doesn't want

to report it, though. The thief is spending less than she did."

Leroy gave a shout of laughter. Relieved, Hilary joined in and, laughing, they entered the apartment together.

Leroy stopped laughing when he saw the man and woman sitting in the sumptuous living room. They were silent, a pair of wax statues, the man reading a newspaper, the woman's head bent over her needlepoint . . . But they weren't statues, they were real. The man looked up from his paper with a startled frown; the woman's hand, holding the needle, stopped in midair.

"Hi, Daddy," said Hilary coolly, "this is Leroy." She took him by the hand and led him past them and into her room. "Homework," she called over her shoulder as she closed the door.

A weird feeling came over Leroy as he stepped into the princess' bower. He felt manipulated as if he were being used for his shock value. In a flash he saw that Hilary had brought him home as a slap in the face to her father and especially to her stepmother. She was rubbing their noses in her freedom to do whatever would most offend them.

When I'm a great dancer this will never happen to me. I'll be famous—I'll be courted and flattered, welcomed everywhere. A white-hot flame burned behind Leroy's eyes, a determination to get so far ahead of the rest of them that they'd see only his taillights. He saw the high mountain, and the tallest peak on that mountain, and himself on that tallest peak. Color didn't matter up there, or where you came from or how you talked—what mattered was who had the talent. No one could take advantage of you if you were on that peak.

Leroy was grateful to Hilary for pointing the way; if he hadn't been so angry, he wouldn't have flashed on it. But he wasn't grateful enough to stay. He pulled his hand out of hers and left the room, slamming the door in her startled face. Without a word to the Van Dorens, he ran out the front door of the apartment. He didn't wait for the elevator, but bounded down the marble staircase two steps at a time, heedless of his dancer's feet and ankles. When he reached the pavement, he turned uptown and began to run. Running and running, he didn't stop until he reached 97th Street. There he saw black faces all around him, and he slowed to a walk, panting. Now he felt cleaner.

Doris and Montgomery sat aghast, faces frozen in shock and horror, as they listened to Ralph's broken recital of what had happened. The boy's words were often muffled by weeping, but the impact of them was not lost. It was a horror story, familiar in the headlines, but devastatingly strange when it happened to someone you knew.

Last night, they had rehearsed late, and Ralph didn't get home at his usual hour. His mother had worked overtime at the factory, and that left Ralph's two sisters alone in the apartment. Doris was shocked at the realization that these were the two "chicks" Ralph had always bragged he lived with—Elena and Teresa, ages five and eleven.

The two girls had been watching television, waiting for Raul or Mamacita. Whoever came home first would feed them, and they'd get a cuddle before bedtime. Elena and Ralph were each other's favorite; he always made her laugh. So, when she'd heard footsteps outside the apartment door, she had hopped off the sofa and gone to look. She was too young to heed Raul's repeated warning: never unlock the door for anybody. Never. Mama and me, that's the only people you let in the apartment. Hear me? She pushed open the door and called to him. Raul? Raul?

No answer, but there was a sound coming from the stairwell. Maybe he was hiding there to tease her. Maybe he'd brought her something to surprise her. Some candy, maybe, or even a little doll. Raul? she asked into the darkness, *es tu?*

It wasn't Raul. It was a brutal hand over her little mouth, and a brutal hand tearing at her body. When the hands finally released her, she screamed and sobbed, crouched on the stairs, until Teresa came.

When Raul had found them in the church, the children crying, his mother praying, he'd gone berserk. Why wasn't she with a doctor instead of a priest? What kind of world was it that attacked five-year-old babies? Hugging the sobbing Elena fiercely to him, he dragged her out of the church, hurling curses at the priest for not sending them to a doctor right away.

The terrible narrative came to a stop at last, and Ralph's sobs began to abate. Montgomery and Doris stared at each other, powerless to give any help.

"Is she all right?" whispered Doris.

"You aren't attacked by some creep at five years old and all right," answered Ralph bitterly.

"I'm sorry," said Doris.

But Ralph's face contorted into anguished guilt. "I wasn't there! I wasn't even there!" he cried.

"What about your father?" Doris asked.

Ralph turned to the window. The Palace Theatre sign threw an evil red light on his face. "We're between fathers," he muttered.

"What does *that* mean?"

Ralph turned and looked at his two friends. He hesitated for a minute, then opened up and let it all spill out. "See, you gotta understand. A Puerto Rican woman . . . she thinks of the kids, you know? And how they gotta have a father. Love and stuff, that's got nothin' to do with it. We got an extra room, and my mom rents it, and the next thing you know . . . a new father. My sister Teresa, she's eleven years old. I tell her it's her fault. Mammi asked her once what she wanted for Christmas, and she said she wanted Papa back. Well, said Mammi, Papa can't come back right now. He's doin' work for the government. But if you'll pray to the Holy Virgin, maybe she'll send you a new Papa for Christmas. I guess someone got the message 'cause our stockings have been full of Papas ever since."

He uttered a short, barking laugh. Doris was stunned. Nothing in her experience of life had taught her that people could live like that. Montgomery said nothing, but his sensitive face showed that he was sharing Ralph's pain.

"They're all right, mostly," Ralph continued. "They stay a few months and help out with the rent and keep the rats out. And I don't mean the animal-type rats

. . . I mean the real thing." His fists balled into hard knots and the veins in his forehead stood out.

"The junkies and the winos and the creeps that set fires, and beat up on little girls . . ." Ralph broke off, and took a gulping breath of air. Then he continued. "I got three sisters, see? One of 'em, María, she's in a special place. We see her a couple times a year. She had some sorta birth defect." He was speaking more and more slowly now, reluctant to face the realities of his troubled life, more reluctant still to face this new need to share them with his friends.

He turned back to the window, staring out, seeing nothing. "No, that's a lie," he said softly. "My father—my real, first, son of a bitch of a father, who ain't no special shit—who's off doing ten in the New York State Penitentiary—he got bothered one night because she was laughin'. I was tellin' some stories . . . just kid stuff, you know . . . flyin' carpets and dragons . . . and he got mad. He always said I was lyin', see . . . and all I was doin' was tellin' stories and makin' my little sisters laugh. And this one night, he just comes down on me like always, and starts beatin' on me . . ."

Doris couldn't help the gasp of pity that escaped her. Ralph turned around and looked at her. She was sitting on the only chair in the room, her face turned to him in the light of the neon.

"Well, an' he's hittin' me, and I keep sayin' that I don't tell lies, I tell *stories,* and I make people laugh and that's a gift, not a goddamn lie and *he* can't do it." The boy's voice rose in pitch until it nearly cracked. "An' he says all right, if he can't *do* it, he can *stop* it, an' my little sister María, she's in the way all of a sudden, and he puts her head inside a wall."

Ralph threw one hand over his eyes to keep back the fresh flood of tears, but there was no containing them. They wet his fingers and slid down his cheeks. The underground river of his heart, with its black, icy waters of experience, had flooded to the surface, and he was weeping openly, a small, thin boy sitting on the windowsill of a huge empty apartment on Broadway, crying a tear for every pain of his young life.

Doris ran to him, and took his hand. Montgomery stood watching them. Through his sobs, Ralph brought the dreadful story to its bitter ending.

"It wasn't a hard wall. Me and my fat head . . . I'da been okay. But . . . María . . . well, she wasn't . . ." He leaned forward and gave himself up to tears. Doris cradled his head in her arms and rocked back and forth as Ralph wept his pain away. She kissed his hair, his eyes, his wet cheeks, and finally his mouth. Soon they were kissing, the two of them crying and kissing at the same time.

Montgomery jammed his hand into the pocket of his jeans and pulled out the keys to the apartment, throwing them on the chair where Ralph would find them. Taking his coat off the hook, he quietly let himself out. He'd have to find somewhere else to sleep tonight.

Ralph and Doris never saw him go.

The time has come, thought Doris, for me to stand up to Mother and tell her I'm a woman. It wouldn't be easy. Doris recognized that all mothers want to keep their children babies, small, cute and dependent, and they will battle to the death against every bit of evidence that baby's growing up. Mrs. Finsecker was the epitome of this. For years she had dressed Doris like a little girl. Any show of independence on the part of her daughter had sent Mrs. Finsecker into hysterics. No mean adversary, she had beaten Doris every round for seventeen years; Doris had never been a match for her.

But with the new confidence she was gaining from her new relationships and her drama work at P.A., Doris felt strong enough to take her mother on again. Ever since freshman year, she had been developing a style of her own, a kind of cross between the street chic of the other girls and her own inner sense of what was right for her. She burrowed into her closet and found a handful of jeans, skirts and jackets that could be combined in new and fashionable ways, and these were what she wore. Her mother protested at all the lovely "little dresses" going to waste, but as Doris hadn't asked for anything new, the rumbles had eventually died down.

But there were other issues between Doris and her mother, far more important and harder to deal with. Shy as she always had been, Doris had dated very little before high school. An occasional movie or birthday party with some nice Jewish boy from the neighborhood had been the sum total of her experience. *And* she'd kept to the ten o'clock curfew imposed by her mother.

But now things were different. How different, Doris was hoping her mother hadn't noticed. But Mrs. Finsecker *had* noticed. Her daughter wasn't bringing Montgomery home anymore, and she no longer talked about him all the time, the way she used to. It had always been: Montgomery thinks . . . or Montgomery told me . . . Such a shame! A fine boy, and Mrs. Finsecker's instincts informed her that Montgomery MacNeill was no "threat" to her lovely daughter.

No, there was someone else, somebody Doris didn't talk about. Somebody Doris didn't bring home to meet her. Therefore—and Mrs. Finsecker's logic was impeccable—he was somebody Doris was ashamed of. *Oy, Gutt*—could it be that Doris was dating a black boy, or worse yet a Puerto Rican? No, impossible. Not my Doris. I brought her up better than that. In the fertile activity of Mrs. Finsecker's mind, there had blossomed an image of Doris—on stage, taking her fifteenth curtain call, clutching large bunches of roses and orchids in her happy arms. Success and fame. Yet somewhere in that fuzzy image lurked the figure of a properous Jewish doctor who would round out her baby's life by making her a good husband. She had never attempted to put the two visions together into one, but fame and marriage remained intertwined in her mother's vision of Doris's future.

What they hadn't discussed was the night she hadn't come home until morning. Doris had tiptoed in the door, hardly breathing or making a sound, and had headed straight for her room. She was afraid of waking her mother up! As if Naomi Finsecker could shut even one eye when her baby was out on the town with God-knows-who! But she had kept her mouth shut, watching and waiting. Disapproval was a new stance for her to take against Doris. Her nagging aside, she knew that Doris had always been such a *good* child. Now Mrs. Finsecker cursed the day she'd dragged her to that audition at Performing Arts. It seemed to be teaching her an independence that was both frightening and loathsome.

Eventually, of course, they had to deal with Doris's changes. Both of them put the discussion off as long as possible; both pretended that nothing had happened, that Doris had never stayed out all that fateful night.

But it was bound to come out, because the two of them were thinking about little else. Doris's mind was on Ralph, and she hugged her newfound tender feelings to herself, wondering if this was the love that all the popular songs were written about. Meanwhile, her mother kept a narrowed eye on Doris at all times, wondering who the adolescent monster was who was leading her baby astray.

About two weeks after the night that Ralph had broken down and wept in Montgomery's apartment, Doris's moment came. She and her mother had gone into downtown Brooklyn to shop. Abraham & Straus was having a sale on designer jeans, and Doris had been coveting a pair. Her mother had promised, her father had shelled out the money, and the two of them had spent a happy day picking out some new things for Doris to wear. It was slightly traumatic, of course, since everything Doris selected was too old for her, according to Mrs. Finsecker, and everything her mother chose was what babies wore, according to Doris. By the end of the Saturday afternoon a compromise had been reached, and now the two of them, lugging bundles and shopping bags, happily made their way up the steps to the elevated platform.

It had turned out to be such a good day that Doris decided to spring something on her mother, something that had been preying on her mind for some time now. Junior year was almost over; in September, Doris would be a senior. Now she knew for certain what she wanted to do. She was going to be a professional actress, and no amount of rejection would discourage her. But who ever heard of an actress named Doris Finsecker? Actresses were supposed to be the most glamorous creatures on earth, and "Doris Finsecker" was like a pail of cold water dumped on all that glamour. Doris had decided to change her name. For this she needed her mother's permission, and now seemed as good a time as any to try for it.

"Mama, I want to change my name."

"What are you talking about?" asked Mrs. Finsecker predictably.

"I want to take a professional name, and I want it to be legal," Doris said as assertively as she dared.

Mrs. Finsecker's jaw dropped, but she recovered brilliantly.

"Barbra Streisand didn't change *her* name," she pointed out.

"Barbra Streisand didn't have a name like Doris Finsecker."

Her mother was shaking her head. "I'll call you Doris like I always have," she stated firmly.

"I won't answer."

"Doris is a perfectly good name," argued Mrs. Finsecker.

"For a perfectly good person. A skinny, boring, nondescript, perfectly good person."

Mrs. Finsecker's eyebrows rose. "I have lots of friends named Doris, and they're none of those things."

"But they're . . ." began Doris, and broke off, biting her lip.

"What? They're what? Go ahead, I want to hear what my daughter thinks is wrong with my friends." Mrs. Finsecker turned an aggrieved eye on Doris, and shifted the heavy shopping bags with an air of injury.

Doris took a deep breath. "I don't want a middle-aged name," she said firmly. Then, rather airily she added, "I can't relate to it. Call me . . . Dominique."

"That's ridiculous," her mother snorted.

"It's French," Doris informed her.

"I know what it is. It isn't you." Mrs. Finsecker stalked to the edge of the platform and checked to see if the train was coming. It wasn't.

"I'll grow into it," said Doris.

Mrs. Finsecker shook her head in disgust. "Dominique *Finsecker?*" she inquired nastily.

"Dominique Dupont."

Mrs. Finsecker screwed up her face in an expression of distaste. "It sounds like a hooker."

"Mama!" gasped Doris.

"I don't know what happened to you," said her mother, shifting ground in an all-out frontal attack. "Can you tell me what happened? Where did my Doris go?"

"Something wonderful happened, Mother. I grew up."

"You became someone else."

"I became an actress."

For one wild moment Doris had an impulse to tell her mother about Ralph, about how she felt when they were together. After all, her mother had been seventeen once herself, hadn't she? She wanted to confide in her, and ask her a million questions about the new feelings that were confusing her heart. But she knew better. How could she make her mother understand that a boy like Ralph, a boy from the south Bronx, who spoke English like a Dead End Kid, was a superior, tender person? If her mother ever met Ralph, all she would see was an undernourished Peurto Rican boy with wild black eyes. And that would be all she'd want to see.

Now Mrs. Finsecker turned on the drama. She dropped her bundles, placed one hand on her ample bosom, approximately over the heart, and with anguish in her voice worthy of a daytime soap opera said, "But I want you to be the Doris who I know, who I love, who helps me with the groceries and makes me birthday cards out of Cheerios boxes, not Dominique who stays out all night."

It was a low blow and it made Doris angry. "Now, Mama . . ." she began.

"And who has the baby or the abortion, God forbid?" demanded Mama. "Not Dominique. She's probably too smart. But Doris, she's dumb enough to get knocked up."

Doris's anger mingled now with embarrassment, for she was still haunted by the pale ghost of shame. Even Dominique Dupont hadn't given up her virginity lightly, nor without second and even third thoughts. "Mama, it was just one night," she protested feebly.

"One night is all it takes," said Mrs. Finsecker, on sure ground now. She knew that the battle, once joined, would be fought over and over. Doris would have to go to war for every scrap of her independence, and she'd have to pay for it with her own blood. But Mrs. Finsecker was intelligent enough, under all her melodrama, to see that it was a war that could have only one outcome . . . eventually Doris would win. Eventually the little girl would really grow up and be able to make a life on her own. It was sad for the parent, but natural for the child.

The train pulled into the station. There were no seats; they would have to stand. They balanced their bundles and bags with tired sighs. Silently, each wrapped in her own thoughts, they began the long ride home.

Doris's mother was right. One night *is* all it takes. Although for Hilary Van Doren, it was hardly one night. She and Leroy had been a heavy number for some time now. He fascinated her, so cool. Cooler even than she. And he was so talented; when he moved, everybody watched him. That was star quality. He was the one you looked at, no matter who else was sharing the stage. She had enjoyed the contrast, too. Leroy, black and elemental. Hilary, blond and sophisticated. She loved the way they looked together. Paradoxes appealed to her; absurdities tickled her fancy. But Hilary wasn't tickled to find herself pregnant.

The myth that hip girls don't get knocked up is just

that, a myth. All of Hilary's coolness, all her good looks, even all her money, couldn't stop the course of nature. They'd been careless a few times, and now Hilary was stuck. Leroy had once laconically suggested birth control pills, but Hilary had reacted with horror. Everybody knows the Pill makes you swell up and get fat, and Hilary lived in fear of an extra pound. So of course she hadn't taken the Pill, Leroy had rejected any measures open to him, and here they were.

Or rather, here Hilary was. She saw no reason to involve Leroy in this, even as she saw no reason to tell her parents. Before she'd tell her stepmother and watch that cat smile, she'd dance barefoot over hot coals. As for her father, Hilary thought he'd react with little more than annoyance. That she didn't need. This was her problem, and she'd handle it. She'd go to Harkness Pavilion; the doctors there were excellent. They would probably only keep her overnight. It would be no worse than having a wart removed, easier in fact. And nobody would be the wiser.

She could take care of herself. Everybody knew that about Hilary Van Doren. She was independent, and didn't need anybody. Not a mother or a father or a boyfriend. The only thing that mattered to her was dancing, and even dancing took second place to being the best. Yes, that was really all that was worthwhile—being the best, and having it acknowledged. Being the most famous dancer in the world. Having fame was more important than having love. Wasn't it?

Then why did she feel so alone, and why were the palms of her hands so wet?

And why did she think it was necessary to explain herself to the admitting nurse? Why couldn't she stop talking, stop telling these silly lies? Whom did she think was interested?

"You see," she babbled to the nurse, as she smoothed her thin kidskin gloves over and over and over, "I've been offered this place at the San Francisco Ballet. I haven't told anybody yet but I'm going to take it. I don't care what they think. I'm a good dancer . . . better than good . . . maybe the best in the school. That's not conceit, is it? Just simple honesty. If I stay in New York everyone will think I bought my way into the American Ballet Theatre, and I'm not starving myself to death for Balanchine! Not that I mind doing the corps de ballet bullshit, but I'd sooner do it out of town. I'll pay my dues on the West Coast and come back to New York a star."

Now that she'd told these lies, Hilary flashed on what she had to do. When this . . . matter . . . was over with, she *would* go to San Francisco! To hell with a high school diploma! They'd give her a job, wouldn't they? The San Francisco Ballet must surely have room for a girl who was going to be a star! And even if they didn't, she'd manage somehow. Maybe she could understudy. Or take classes. Or something. There had to be something.

"I've always had this crazy dream of dancing all the classic roles before I'm twenty-one," she told the bored nurse. "I want Giselles and Coppélias coming out of my feet . . . and Sleeping Beauties . . . and the Swan. I want bravos in Stuttgart and Leningrad and Paris and maybe even a ballet created especially for me." She tossed back her heavy mane of bright hair and attempted a smile. It came out too bright, and it faded very quickly, a star in nova. "So, you see . . . there really isn't any room . . . for a baby."

The nurse looked up for the first time. She had almost completed filling out Hilary's application. "Will this be Master Charge or American Express, honey?" she asked.

Fishing in her purse for her American Express card, Hilary felt a shiver run down her back. She felt more alone than ever.

I can't believe it, Doris told herself happily. I must be the only kid in the drama department who hasn't seen *The Rocky Horror Picture Show*. It's taken me three years to get here. It had better be worth the wait. Her excitement began to mount, and she gave Ralph Garcy's arm a squeeze.

Ralph returned her smile indulgently. Sometimes she was just like a little kid. Look at her now, her eyes all big and round, digging this freak show. He wondered what she'd look like if she was ever exposed to a *real* freaky scene, like the ones he'd grown up with. Shit! This was only a movie.

For some reason that nobody had ever really explained *The Rocky Horror Picture Show* had become a cult phenomenon. It had begun life as an experimental live musical, in a tiny theatre in London, in 1973. So successful that it had moved eventually to a five-hundred-seat theatre in Chelsea, it had run for years. Brought to America, it enjoyed a successful run in Los Angeles, and was filmed in 1975. The movie bombed. Apparently, heartland America wasn't ready for a mad scientist in full drag, who creates a "monster," a beautiful blond weight lifter, to cater to his bizarre sexual tastes, and who seduces every warm body—male, female—that crosses his zany path. America wasn't ready, but teenage America was. Around the country, one small theatre after another booked it in to play at midnight. Suddenly, *Rocky Horror* was *the* thing to do on a Saturday night.

But what really made it freaky was that *Rocky* addicts saw the picture not once, not twice, not even fifteen times, but over and over and over again. *Rocky Horror* became for them not merely a movie but a way of life. All week long, they went to school or worked at humdrum jobs, but on the weekends, they came alive.

About ten-thirty on Saturday night, the line began to form outside the Eighth Street Theatre; by ten minutes to midnight, when the doors opened, every seat would be sold. The show actually began on line. *Rocky Horror* freaks would dress up like their favorite characters in the movie—Magenta the maid and Riff Raff the butler seemed to have the largest following—and paint their faces in lurid masks. These people—the regulars in costume—didn't have to wait in line; they were the first people allowed in the theatre, and they often got in free. But, like visiting royalty, they allowed the peasants to see them, wafting down the line to greet old friends.

"Loose joints, loose joints. Get high before you see the show."

Doris gasped. She had never seen grass sold openly on the streets before, but here was a tall young man with long blond hair, dressed like a bizarro in a white tailcoat and sequins, hawking dope to the masses, a reefer at a time. When he came up to them, making his pitch, Ralph gave him a look that said, Puh-leeeeze. As though Ralph Garcy would sink so low as to buy a reefer off a stranger!

"Are all the people here looney tunes?" Doris whispered to Ralph.

"Are you kidding?" Ralph shot back. "This is nothing, *nada*. Wait until we get inside."

Once inside, Ralph propelled Doris at a run down the aisle toward the front of the theatre. Everybody seemed to want to sit as close to the screen as possible, which Doris couldn't understand. The three front rows had already been taken by the people in *Rocky Horror* costume, who were spread out over all the chairs as though they were home in their living rooms. Which, in a sense, they were.

Doris had been afraid that Ralph was going to show up in his full Tim Curry Frank-N-Furter drag, the one he'd worn at school last year, and it was with relief that she saw his jeans and T-shirt when they'd met in front of the theatre, even though his T-shirt bore the legend, "Disregard Previous T-Shirt." Doris was proud of her new blouse, real silk, purchased on sale at A&S.

But now as she looked around the theatre, she realized that she and Ralph were underdressed. In fact, they looked almost middle-aged compared to what she saw around them. Those boys and girls who weren't in costumes from the movie were wearing getups even more grotesque—glitter pasted on cheeks and brows, green lipstick and nail polish (on the boys), hair dyed in outlandish colors, trailing silks and satins and sleazy threadbare velvets. It looks like All Fools' Day in medieval England, said Doris to herself.

But when a naked boy came striding up the aisle selling posters, Doris jumped in her seat. On second glance—and she could hardly bring herself to take that second glance—she could see he was not completely naked. He was wearing a small . . . something . . . around his hips that kept him legal if not modest. It was a cross between a large diaper and a small loincloth. The boy's body had been oiled a startling shade of gold, to match his dyed hair. The effect was startling and even rather beautiful, unless you looked too closely.

The golden boy wasn't the only one selling something. Doris became aware that the movie theatre was a hive of activity, with "Riff Raffs" and "Magentas" of all sizes and shapes running up and down the aisles trying to get people to buy chances on a raffle, or programs, or the sound track of the movie on records or tapes. The only one not selling anything was Frank-N-Furter himself, a tall boy or girl (it was difficult for Doris to tell) who stood languidly down front, over to one side, leaning against a wall and toking on a large reefer rolled in banana paper. Apparently, as the star of the show, he felt it unseemly to lower himself to commercialism; besides, he was too stoned to collect money.

The atmosphere in the theatre was that of a carnival, and Doris found it exhilarating. By now, it was well past midnight; yet there seemed to be no sign of a movie. The curtain hadn't even been drawn back from the screen. Doris felt as though she was at a big party that had been going on for several years, and to which she had just been invited.

Suddenly a man appeared in front of the screen. He wore a greasy, threadbare tuxedo and his hair was plastered down with Vaseline, giving him the look of a Chicago gangster, Prohibition period. The audience seemed to recognize him, because cheers and whistles and the stomping of feet greeted his appearance. He held up his hands for silence.

"Welcome to the *Rocky Horror* at the Eighth Street. Let's have a big hand for . . . *Christine,* who is here tonight for her one hunnerd and fiftieth show!"

More cheers from the audience as a plump blond girl happily mounted the stage to get her badge, marking her as an official *Rocky Horror* groupie.

"Get on with the show!" yelled a heckler from one of the back rows.

"We *are* the show!" yelled back the master of ceremonies, and the audience went wild, chanting, "Yeah, yeah, yeah!"

"If you don't like it, go see the show on Staten Island."

"Yeah. Yeah. Yeah."

Doris's eyes were as round as dinner plates, but Ralph, who'd seen it all before, just sat back and took it all in. Reaching into his jeans pocket, he withdrew a joint and lit it up. He passed it to Doris, but she shook her head no. She had never tasted marijuana, and her mother's warning still rang in her ears.

Up on the stage, announcements were made, the raffle was held and a small kid who spent every waking moment thinking about *The Rocky Horror Picture Show* carried an original poster from the first London production back to his seat with an expression of bliss on his face. The "cast" was introduced, and each of them took a bow to enthusiastic applause.

And then, at about twelve thirty-five, the lights went down, the curtains parted, the screen was revealed and the movie finally got under way.

Doris had known she was in for an unusual experience, but she never imagined that a live "cast" would act out every gesture and every line in sync with what was happening on the screen. Nor had she expected that the audience would talk back to the movie. And with funny lines, yet. It was as though they had a script; the entire audience spoke the same wisecrack at the same time. Dammit, they *did* have a script, a memorized script. Doris had never seen anything like it. When the couple left the church in the movie, in a shower of rice, half the audience put up black umbrellas and the other half pelted them with rice. Doris's own hair was suddenly heavy with rice. Laughing, she shook it out.

When Brad and Janet read the sign on the iron gate—*Enter At Your Own Risk!!*—Ralph reached for another joint and lit it. Once more he offered it to Doris, who refused it again. But this time he pressed it on her and, curious, she took a tentative puff, and then another.

She wasn't sure what she expected from the grass, but there was no sudden rush or disorientation. In fact, she felt nothing except a mild constriction of the scalp, as though she were wearing a tight French beret. But in a little while she found herself laughing harder than ever—everything was so *funny!*—and she suddenly thought that she'd never had such a good time in her life as she was having now. Her mouth felt a little dry, and she had a sudden craving for a Coca-Cola—sweet and cold and very wet. Everything was so funny!

Janet and Brad were in Frank-N-Furter's castle now, being leered at by the evil Riff Raff. And it was time to do the Time Warp, a jump to the left and then a step to the right.

In the theatre, the line was forming for the Time Warp. Boys and girls were running toward the stage and forming a line, jumping and hopping like the mad Transylvanians on the screen behind them.

Doris giggled wildly. That looked like so much fun! Although the grass was working on her head, something else was building up inside her, had been for some time. Impulsively, she stood up. She was heading down the aisle when she remembered her brand-new silk blouse. Suddenly, the most important thing in the world became that blouse, and not getting it soiled. I'll take it off, she said to herself. Carefully she removed the blouse and handed it to the astonished Ralph. Then she ran to the stage and wriggled into the line, totally un-self-conscious. Bathed in the dim light from the screen, Doris looked fully dressed in her satin camisole. Fully dressed and very pretty, thought Ralph. Her face was so animated it looked especially beautiful, and she seemed to be having the time of her life, dancing and singing as though she was the star of some cosmic musical. That's my chick, he thought proudly.

Thus Doris Finsecker, stoned and liberated, made her first appearance on any public stage.

On Monday, Doris couldn't wait to get to school and tell Montgomery all about her evening at *The Rocky Horror Picture Show*. But Montgomery proved elusive; if she hadn't known better, she'd have sworn he was avoiding her. At last she trapped him at their locker between classes, and got him to promise to meet her and Ralph after school at Joe Allen's.

Montgomery had been avoiding Doris, even though he couldn't explain why. He supposed it was jealousy. Ever since Ralph and Doris had become a couple, Montgomery was feeling extra and in the way. Their double happiness made his single misery look even more miserable. Together, they were doing things that he and Doris used to do. Wasn't it he who was supposed to take Doris to *The Rocky Horror Picture Show* last year? Instead, she had gone with Ralph while he had sat alone in his apartment, staring out the window at the garishly lit street below, picking out a melancholy tune on his Martin guitar. Some big evening!

Inside, of course, Montgomery knew he was being foolish. There was nothing to prevent him from spending time with them. He could no doubt have gone along with them on Saturday. Or, better still, he could have found himself a date. But shyness always prevented him from making new friends. It was his own fault he'd been home alone, not Doris's and not Ralph's.

The trouble with me, thought Montgomery, is that

I'm too damn serious. I analyze everything, and I want everything to come out even. I'm looking for answers in places where there aren't even any questions. What I need is to have fun.

Sitting with Ralph and Doris at Joe Allen's, Montgomery heard about the fun he'd missed. Doris, extremely proud of her accomplishment, had embellished the telling only a little bit, but Montgomery was left with the impression that she had dropped acid and taken off every stitch in front of an audience of six thousand people.

"You did what?" he asked.

"I smoked a joint, took off my blouse and danced the Time Warp," said Doris, pleased with herself.

"I'm telling you, you wouldn't believe it. It was incredible!" Ralph leaned forward over the butcher block table, his eyes glowing.

"It was more than incredible," interrupted Doris. "It was fun. And it wasn't only the grass. It was me, the way *I* felt. I always felt naked when people looked at me. But those people weren't looking at me. They were looking at someone I put on, like a costume. If I don't have a personality of my own . . . so what? I'm an actress. I can put on as many personalities as I want!"

Smiling, Montgomery lifted his glass of milk, "To schizophrenia."

"Fuckin' right." Doris smiled, clinking her glass against his. She looked around the restaurant proudly.

Joe Allen's was a favorite hangout for junior and senior students at Performing Arts, when they could afford it. A theatre bar, located near Shubert Alley, it was impossible to get into on matinee days and when the shows let out. You saw all kinds of celebrities going in for chili and hamburgers. Doris had once caught a glimpse of Dustin Hoffman, and once Richard Burton had smiled at her as he came out. But now, at five o'clock in the afternoon, the place was only lightly sprinkled with patrons. It looked like every side-street theatre hangout near Times Square—red brick walls, daily specials chalked up on a big blackboard, plants hanging from the ceiling, and handsome waiters.

It was a handsome waiter who approached them now.

"You kids ready to order?" he asked efficiently.

Doris looked up at him and her look became a stare. Her mouth made a little "O" of surprise. "Michael?"

"Yeah?" said the waiter curiously.

"You don't remember?" breathed Doris.

Michael Lambert appeared confused. There was something familiar about the girl, but he couldn't place the face, or those of the boys sitting with her.

"Two years ago. I'm Doris Fins . . . I *was* Doris Finsecker. When you were a senior. At P.A."

"Oh, yeah, yeah, sure," said Michael, on familiar ground now. "Around the corner." This was another of those babies who'd had a crush on him. He didn't remember the girl, but he hadn't forgotten the type.

"And you remember Montgomery MacNeill? And Ralph Garcy?"

"Yeah, yeah. Sure. The good old days, right?"

"Right," said Montgomery, understanding that Michael had only the vaguest notion of who they were.

"How was Hollywood?" asked Doris breathlessly.

Now Michael was looking a little uncomfortable. "Slow," he said stiffly. "I met some people. I went to some parties. I did a pilot for a series."

"I didn't see it," said Doris mournfully.

"Nobody saw it," said Michael with a wry twist of his handsome lips.

"I'm sorry," said Doris.

"I played a male nurse for two days. On a soap."

"Oh."

Michael shook his head to clear it of bitter memories. "I didn't like L.A."

There was no mistaking his tone. "Are you studying?" asked Doris quickly, to change the subject. She didn't notice the embarrassed expressions on the faces of Montgomery and Ralph. They knew the score, and it was L.A. 5, Michael 0.

"Oh, I catch a class here and there." Michael's answer was deliberately vague. "When I can. Hard times, you know. I read for a showcase. I got a big call-back coming up next week . . ." He broke off, feeling like an idiot.

By now even Doris had caught on. She cast her eyes down, sick at heart, feeling so terribly sorry for Michael, and somehow a little sorry for herself too. A silence fell among them.

"Yeah," said Michael, as briskly as he could. "Well, what are you kids having? We got a special today on the fried clams . . ."

Doris hated clams, but she felt Michael's discomfort so deeply that she couldn't find it in her heart to be responsible for any further rejection, no matter how trivial. "Uh . . . clams sound good," she said lamely.

"Yeah, clams," mumbled Ralph.

"I'll have the clams," said Montgomery, who didn't like them any more than Doris.

"Clams all around, then," said Michael, collecting the menus. Without meeting their eyes again, he left to put in their order.

Doris could barely choke down her lunch; she was torn between pity for Michael and revulsion for the clams. The three of them ate quickly, in silence, paid the check, and got out of there as quickly as they could.

Once out on the street, Doris drew in large, noisy gulps of the evening air. Although Ralph seemed to notice nothing, Montgomery sensed that Doris was in a highly emotional state. He moved to the girl's side and put one arm protectively over her shoulder.

At his touch, she burst out, her voice shaking with feeling, "If Michael Lambert . . . he was the handsomest . . . the best . . . If Michael Lambert . . . he got Best Actor at graduation . . . William *Morris* signed him . . . If Michael *Lambert* couldn't make it, *how can I?*"

"Hey, hey," Montgomery said quietly, giving her shoulder a squeeze. "Hey, come *on!*" He turned their footsteps east, toward Broadway and his apartment. All the way there, he held Doris to his side, telling her over and over that everything would be all right.

Upstairs, Montgomery lit a tall candle and set out a bottle of American wine and three glasses. They sat around on the mattress, while Doris pulled herself together, taking long swallows of the sharp wine. Soon she was calmer.

"You know, all my life I've seen guys like Michael Lambert come and go," began Montgomery. Doris looked at him, open-mouthed. "Oh, yes," he reassured her, "there was a Michael Lambert in almost every one of my mother's plays, a young guy who could act a little and look impressive. They're called juveniles. If you have a nickel, you could buy six of them. Doris, they're not stars, they're candles. They don't give off a lot of light. Just like this baby here." He gestured toward the candle they were sitting around. Its light was wavering and flickering. "Pretty, right? But you can't work by it or read by it. Doris, that has nothing to do with you or me or Ralph here. We're not pretty people, but we have something better going for us."

"Speak for yourself," cracked Ralph. "I'm pretty people."

"Oh, Ralph, be serious for a minute. Go on, Montgomery."

"Look, all that ease and self-confidence of Michael's, that's probably his worst enemy. Everything in life has been handed to him on a plate, garnished with watercress. Now I'm not saying that every artist has to suffer and starve, but pain helps, Doris, it really does. No true artist can ever be really comfortable. There's always an anxiety gnawing at him or her, not only the desire to be the best, but the need. You can't be the best without that need. And stars are the best. That's all it is."

"Well, then we're guaranteed. I hurt the most so I'm the biggest star, right?" Grinning, Ralph looked around the group.

"Maybe," said Montgomery slowly, choosing to take Ralph's words literally. "Maybe you are. But there are no guarantees, Ralph. Just a lot of hard work, and a lot of rejection coming up. And you have to be strong, not only for the rejections, but for the success, too. Fame really takes it out of you. I know. I've seen it up close and it doesn't come free."

Doris leaned forward, her chin on her hand. "I guess I don't know anything about rejection. Not really. My mother's been behind me pushing all my life. But at least that's encouragement. My family is kind of like a security blanket. It may get too hot sometimes, and you may want to push it off, but it's always there. And it keeps you warm. I wonder . . . if I ever got to be famous, I mean really famous, would I know how to handle it?"

"Just keep an eye on me, Baby," Ralph told her. "I'll teach you how to handle it. You ride around in a big, customized Dorado, white leather upholstery, shiny red paint, stereo tape deck, four speakers, bar in the back. Everybody knows your face, and when you want something, they jump. 'Yes-sir-no-sir-whatever-you-wish-sir.' " Ralph stood up and began bowing from the waist, imitating future flunkies. Doris and Montgomery couldn't help smiling.

"Can I get you something, sir? The key to Fort Knox? The President's daughter? The cover of *Time* magazine?"

Doris shook her head, even though she was giggling. "Ralph, that's not your fame, that's Freddie Prinze's."

"So what's wrong with that?" demanded Ralph.

"Well," Doris's lovely face was serious. "You have to take what belongs to *you*, not to somebody else. And you have to earn it yourself, because you are what you are. Isn't that what Mr. Farrell keeps trying to get us to understand? To be ourselves, to work with our *selves*, our own feelings and needs and desires?"

"Yes, that's exactly it," said Montgomery.

"So, I guess I was stupid to get so upset over Michael Lambert. He's him, and I'm me, and we just don't have the same things to offer."

"Uh huh," Montgomery agreed.

"But what if the world doesn't want what I offer either?" Doris looked beseechingly at both of them.

"Those are the chances we took when we started," Montgomery answered. "Those are the chances we take every day we're in the theatre. We just have to keep on trying harder, I guess. Keep on making the offer."

"Me, I want it all," Ralph announced. "I want them to love me, to respect me, and to laugh when I tell them to. I want the fast cars and sharp clothes, and those flashbulbs going off in my face."

"I'd hate that, I think," said Montgomery.

Doris thought about it for a second. "I'd probably hate it, too. But then, if I ever had it, and for some reason it stopped, I'd probably hate that even more."

And suddenly they were laughing together, and the anxieties had lifted, blown away like the thin smoke of the candle flame. At least for now.

SENIOR YEAR

1

THE pinnacle. The top of the heap. With three years behind them, they came into the senior year the lords and owners of the school. Now they could look with tolerant amusement at the terrified freshmen peeping around corners and tiptoeing in the corridors. How far they had come from those baby days. They were taller, stronger, more skillful and much less frightened.

Less frightened maybe of what lay behind them, but there was still the world outside, just waiting its turn. Senior year was at once a challenge and a refuge, a place to hide out until it was time to face Life. Senior year was the last bastion of childhood, and they intended to make the most of its protection.

For the first time, they were treated with a respect akin to awe. The freshmen and sophomores considered them something between the faculty and the gods. The faculty had to admit that anybody making it through the first three years was probably pulling his weight, and teachers' attitudes, for the most part, became a bit softer. Not that the seniors didn't have to work. No, if anything they worked harder than ever. But there was an air of collaboration and trust about every assignment. As though the teachers were saying, You and I know so much, here's what *we* ought to do.

By the senior year, they were all supposed to be accustomed to performing. The Senior Show was the biggest event of the school year, and every department would be fully involved. Every senior's input was required. With some supervisory help from the faculty, they were to do everything themselves—write the sketches and the music, choreograph the dances, produce and direct. It would take them the entire school year to get it together and polish it to a near-professional shine, but they would be ready. This was something they'd worked for, dreamed about for three long years. They'd be ready.

It was also time to think about the next step in life. Where would they go? What would they be doing? For some, high school graduation would lead on naturally to college.

Montgomery, for example, was not even certain that he was going to be an actor. Working with Doris and Ralph, he'd discovered his own talent for directing. He loved envisioning a piece of theatre and bringing the vision to reality. And there was playwriting, too. Unknown even to Doris, a manuscript was growing next to his typewriter, almost as though he'd planted it there. So far he had only one act and part of the second; maybe it wasn't even very good, but it occupied much of his thoughts and it kept him from loneliness. Montgomery wanted four more years of school. He needed them. His first choice was Yale Drama School, but the competition for places there was fierce, and he might not make it. Even so, he'd go on to college. It was something that both he and his mother agreed on.

Doris, too, expected to go to college. She'd heard Montgomery speak of Yale, and a sweet longing filled her for New Haven. It sounded like paradise, college and drama school combined. But Doris was more practical than that. There was no way the Finsecker family could spring for Yale. She'd have to settle for Brooklyn College, which would give her a college degree, while she made the rounds of Off-Off-Off-Broadway hoping for theatrical experience.

Bruno was heading for the Juilliard College of Music. Even Mr. Shorofsky acknowledged it. Mama would have to wait a little while longer for her six mink coats, but it would be worth it. Bruno Martelli fully expected to be bigger than Elton John.

For Coco, Leroy and Ralph, college was a foreign word. Coco was so eager to get out into the world and start knocking it dead that no power on earth could get her back into a schoolroom once she got her high school diploma. Leroy was only glad he'd made it this far; any more learning and his head would explode. Besides, he lived for only one thing, to dance. He intended to be famous, as famous as Misha Baryishnikov—he would be a real Black Russian. Only he wouldn't waste his time on ballet—the kind of dancing he wanted to do was strictly his own. Miss Berg had some ideas for him, places she planned to send him to . . . *if* he could keep up his average and not flunk English.

As for Ralph, he was getting itchy. Very itchy. It seemed to him that he'd already served his time at P.A. After all, Freddie didn't graduate, did he? Yeah, he'd learned a lot from Mr. Farrell. At first, he'd thought it was all shit, but he'd soon come to see that there was no jivin' behind it. Those exercises of Farrell's, loco as they'd seemed, had sharpened his timing and given him insight, two things a successful comic needs.

But Ralph felt ready. Another year of school was a waste of time as far as he could see. Oh, he wasn't dropping out. No sense doing that . . . yet. He had no place to go except back to the delivery cart at the A&P. Besides, Doris was at P.A., and seeing her every day was the brightest part of his life. But he had plans. And they didn't include taking College Boards.

. .No, Ralph was going to get the jump on all of them. He planned to showcase himself. He loved that word "showcase." It made him feel like something precious under glass.

There was, in New York, a number of cafes which have built their reputations on presenting new comics. They do this by holding what used to be called "amateur nights" but now are called "showcases." Anybody can get up there, provided he has the guts to do it and some material not too obviously stolen from established comedians. On the whole, they're friendly places, willing to give a kid a break.

What you do is go down there on a Monday afternoon, and wait in line until you get a number. They pick thirty or thirty-five gals and guys to go on that

218

night. They'll hand out maybe forty numbers, in case a few get stage fright and don't show up. And you go on that night in the order your number is called. You got maybe five, maybe six minutes to make it or break it. The smart comic knows that nothing stimulates laughter like people laughing, and he'll bring his brothers, his sisters, even his old lady—anybody to start the laughing so that he comes off funny. If he's asked back, he's in. A number of famous funny people got their start that way, and a much larger number of people you never heard of died at one of those Monday nights.

Ralph didn't know that you should bring a claque with you, but when Doris found out he was going to play Catch a Rising Star she went berserk with pride, and half the senior drama class showed up, plus some of the musicians and dancers. They sat at the crowded wooden tables with the checkered cloths, nursing one beer or a couple of Cokes, waiting for their buddy to kill the people.

Doris was particularly happy that evening, and she glowed. When she looked like that, she was right next to beautiful, thought Montgomery, looking at her fondly. Not only was Doris proud of Ralph, she was pretty proud of herself, too. She had applied to a number of colleges, even though she'd expected all along to go to Brooklyn College. That morning she had received an acceptance from the drama school at Juilliard, in Lincoln Center. And her mother told her she could go! After all, she'd be in New York, and she'd still be living at home. As it turned out, Mrs. Finsecker had been scrimping and stinting for years, saving money for Doris's college education. So even the money was there.

It was too much! Alive with happiness, Doris could barely focus her attention on the young master of ceremonies who was clutching the microphone and shading his eyes against the light, an old comic's trick.

"Welcome to Catch a Rising Star, ladies and gentlemen. Who's here for the first time?" He peered into the audience.

A number of hands went up, and Montgomery prodded Doris to raise her hand. The MC counted the house.

"Who's here for the last time?" he quipped.

A few polite chuckles greeted this chestnut. "You're a fabulous audience," he told them. "You've got great control. Well, as some of you know, this is Monday night. Monday night, the night the new talent comes out. Some of these kids have never been on a stage before, and some of them never will be again. But maybe you're lucky tonight. Gabriel Kaplan started out here, and so did Jimmie Walker and David Brenner and Freddie Prinze, and maybe tonight's gonna start a career for somebody. You never can tell."

The Performing Arts kids leaned forward in anticipation, and Montgomery gave Doris's hand an encouraging squeeze. A couple of tables away, Coco checked the place out curiously. Was this something for her, too? She decided against it. With all she had going for her, why sweat a comic act? She'd stick to the singing and the dancing and the acting. She gave Bruno a wide sweet smile, and he returned it, tightening his arm around her shoulder. They'd been going

220

together three months now, and he was in seventh heaven and heading for eighth.

"And now . . ." the MC was saying, imitating a drum roll, "Number One! And let's give a big hand to this boy. He's been here since noon to get in line . . ." He consulted a slip of paper he was holding. "Ralph Garcy!"

To the sound of applause, Ralph trotted out onto the stage. He was wearing a white denim jacket over a white shirt, and under the lights he looked pale, his eyes bright, black and glittering. But he appeared sure of himself as he took hold of the mike and went into his riff.

"Thank you. Thank you. Like the man said, my name is Ralph Garcy and I'm a professional asshole. I see a few amateurs in the audience. That's always encouraging."

He stopped for laughter, and he heard it. The boys and girls from school were supporting the local talent.

"No, seriously. I have a few friends here tonight." He nodded in the direction of Doris and Montgomery. "It's nice to have friends. Up where I live, in the south Bronx . . . that's the country just north of Harlem and west of Puerto Rico . . . up there you gotta have friends. You can't afford to alienate *any* minority groups, you know? Like the cockroaches. I mean, you gotta respect 'em. They got a good union. Last week fifteen thousand of them marched down my block demanding better housing."

Laughter interrupted him; he saw Doris banging the table in hysterics, while the kids from the music department were falling all over the place. It felt good, it felt good.

"And the rats," he went on. "You don't throw *them* a little something under the table, they get ugly. Last week they stole a building."

Ralph's eyes were glittering more brightly than ever, and two round feverish spots appeared on his cheekbones. He was on a roll and he knew it. He was taking them all the way out, and he'd bring them all the way home. It was power, power like he'd never felt before.

"No, seriously. The security guard went to get something to eat and the building was gone. Really. I love the south Bronx. Everywhere you go from there is up. So everyone's got dreams, see. Big dreams. Now with me, ever since I was a kid, my dreams have been strictly neon. You know, show business. But you stop your average boy on the street in the south Bronx, and ask him what he wants to be when he grows up. Know what he'll say? 'I wanna be an ex-junkie.' Ask your average girl. 'I wanna be a dynamite hooker.' People up there, man, they can't even afford empty dreams."

Looking out over the audience, Ralph told himself, they're mine. They belong to me tonight, and I can do anything I want with them. He loved them, singly and collectively, loved their faces, the sound of their laughter, loved where they were coming from. Because they were loving him.

"But you gotta have dreams, even in the south Bronx. And people do, all kinds of dreams. You can see 'em right on the street. In fact, it's a problem drivin' on account of so many dreams on the street being seen by coke-heads." Giggles here from the hip ones.

"Soon as that white line is laid down the middle of

the street, some fool dreamer follows behind with a straw and snorts it up." He gave a little sniff, and the house went crazy.

"And then there's sex. Kids are into sex a lot earlier in the south Bronx . . . like 6 A.M. No, seriously, folks, I know an eight-year-old in my building who has her own apartment . . . dates junior executives . . . goes to singles bars . . . she had a baby girl last week, who was *born* pregnant. Anyway, you grow up fast in the south Bronx. You don't have time for fairy tales, you know. Or if you do, they got new twists. Remember Little Red Riding Hood? 'Why, Grandma, what big eyes you have'" He mimicked a falsetto. Then he sniffed loudly and wiped at his nose. " 'Here, sugar,'" he gruffed, " 'You try some of this, an' your eyes gonna get big, too.' "

The kids at Doris's table were howling, but the MC was making throat-cutting motions in the wings, to tell Ralph that he was going overtime and he'd better cut it short.

"Hey, I gotta go now," he told his happy audience. "But I wanna tell you you're all great. My mother thanks you, my father thanks you, my sisters thank you, my brothers thank you, the winos thank you, the junkies thank you, the narcs thank you, the rats thank you, the roaches thank you and I thank you." With one hand over his heart, Ralph bowed deeply and ran off the stage.

He was streaming sweat; his white denim jacket was wet through. The red spots on his cheeks were so bright they appeared painted on, and his eyes were twin laser beams. Doris ran to him and threw her arms around him, kissing him hard, but Montgomery

223

stood in the doorway of the tiny communal dressing room and took a good look at Ralph. It was more than excitement that was making Ralph glow. The flush of success was redder because of some chemical or other. Speed, probably, Montgomery decided. Uppers were making Ralph so talkative. Look at him now, he was so ripped, he couldn't stop. Well, who could blame him, his first time on a stage? But it was no good for an actor to depend on artificial stimulants . . . the excitement had to come from within. Still, he knew better than to say anything. This was certainly Ralph's evening. He'd worked hard for it and he'd earned it. Success. It was wonderful, enviable. So why wasn't Montgomery envious? Why did he have this foreboding, looking at Ralph? He was afraid of saying anything; he didn't want to bring Ralph down.

Ralph didn't want to stay on for the other sets, he was too wired. Bouncing out front, he thanked the kids, grabbed Doris and they split.

All the way to the subway, he couldn't stop talking. Like his mouth was a train and it was hurtling down a hill without any brakes. Doris had never seen him like this. His energy was ferocious, even though it was obvious to her that he was wiped out, totally drained and exhausted. Still, he managed to keep it going.

"You were wonderful," she told him for the third time.

"Naaaahhhh," said Ralph for the third time.

"Yes, really."

Ralph nodded. He knew it. "I was good. I felt good. I felt more than good and they want me back."

"They do?" said Doris, her eyes growing round.

"The guy's got another club on the Island and they want to book me regular," he told her with real pride.

"That's wonderful," said Doris in a small voice. She wasn't quite sure how she felt about this. All she knew was that a subway platform was hardly the right place to discuss life decisions.

"That isn't just wonderful," said Ralph intensely. "It's real. It's like . . . electricity, you know? You're up there and those faces are out starin' at you and you're leadin' 'em out . . . drawin' them . . . buildin' up a positive charge, like they say . . . and then . . . *bam!* You hit 'em with the juice and they explode and that power goes flowin' back and forth. And it's you that's doin' it to them. You're makin' them laugh. That's the meanest high there is. That beats dope and sex combined! I love acting!"

Doris tried to smile. She heard the Brooklyn train approaching the station, and she tried to think of something to say, but nothing came to mind. She felt down, in contrast to Ralph's being so up. She simply couldn't match his excitement.

Ralph took a sharp look at his girl. The corners of her expressive mouth were turned down, a sure sign she was not happy. And Ralph knew why. He'd been too full of himself, neglecting her entirely. He'd make it up to her. Grabbing her by her shoulders, Ralph planted an enthusiastic kiss on her cheek. His words tumbled out in a rush.

"I think it's great. About your bein' accepted at Juilliard and all. You can study and I'll work the clubs. And with my money, we can get a place. And then . . . after a while . . . we'll get married, maybe. And I'll get a hit series and make twenty thousand a

225

week and the cover of *TV Guide*. And we'll have two kids . . . a boy and a girl. And when they grow up, they'll go to the High School of Performing Arts, like their parents. What do you say?"

Doris had to laugh; she had no other choice. "What about me?" she demanded as the train thundered into the station. "Don't I get a career?"

"Sure!" yelled Ralph over the noise of the subway. "You'll do Shakespeare in the Park and stuff and win seventeen Tony awards. All right?"

The car doors opened, and Ralph pushed Doris into the train, kissing her hard. "Now don't miss your station and don't go mugging or raping anyone. Hear me?"

As the train doors closed, Doris shook her head in resigned amusement. Too much! He was crazed tonight. She had never seen him quite like this before . . . so charged up. So manic. What an insane relationship, she told herself. And she refused to think of the future. But her pride in Ralph's success warmed her all the way to Brooklyn.

Coco Hernandez had lost none of her confidence in herself, none of her determination to see her name up in lights. Fame was still the most important word in her vocabulary. Yet these three and a half years of high school had taught her a few important lessons. She had expected to work hard, but not this hard. She learned that nothing was about to be handed to her, no matter how much sparkle she was putting out.

Nothing replaced practice, nothing took the place of constant rehearsal. Working with Bruno, booking the band, playing the weekend gigs had showed her the less glamorous aspects of show business. And she wasn't too crazy about them.

She knew that she and Bruno could keep Bruno's Black and White Band going all through his college years, but the thought depressed her. After all, how many times could she sing "Hava Nagila"? How many sweet-sixteen birthday parties could they work, where the first request would always be for "Feelings"? One more chorus of "Feelings" and she'd stick her finger down her throat.

No, if Performing Arts had taught her anything, it was that show business, besides hard, grueling work, was often a matter of who you knew as much as what you knew. Contacts. That was the magic word. Three years ago, when she danced through the doors of this high school, Coco Hernandez had no contacts. Now, in her senior year, still no contacts. Somehow she doubted whether all the managers of all the catering establishments in New York, put together, could arrange for one important audition for her.

By now she had performed regularly, in school and out of it. Nobody doubted her talent, but Coco was disheartened whenever she thought of how many talented people in the world weren't working. What Coco needed was to be discovered. One break. Just one break and she'd be off and running, chasing that butterfly of fame with the net of her energy.

As she had done every school morning since freshman year, Coco took her breakfast in the Howard Johnson's on Broadway. She always took the corner table by the window—her "office" as she liked to think of it—and sat there for forty minutes, drinking coffee after coffee and catching up on the trades. *Variety, Backstage, Show Business*—she read them all the way through, every item—from who was flying in from the coast to who was holding an open call for dancers.

She was nose-deep in a story about all the kids who were fired from *Annie* because they were getting too tall when she noticed a man staring at her.

So what else was new? Only this one seemed to be a real creep. Cutting her eyes at him over the top of the paper, Coco checked him out. She didn't like what she saw, and she shifted her position in the chair so that her face was turned away from him. Don't give them anything to look at and they usually stop looking.

Not this one, though. Suddenly, he was beside her, hovering over her table. About thirty or so, he badly needed a shave, his clothes were wrinkled and dirty, and his hands looked as though they had not been on speaking terms with soap and water for days. But it was his eyes that put her off the most, decided Coco, sneaking a peek at him as he dangled over her. They were weirdo eyes—too bright, too shifty. He gave her the shivers.

"Excuse me."

Coco burrowed deeper into *Show Business* and didn't answer. If he persisted, she'd leave. If he followed her, she'd get him in the *cojones* with the pointy toe of her Western boot. He wasn't the first loser she'd dealt with, and he wouldn't be the last.

"I've seen you somewhere," breathed the creep.

228

"Sure," said Coco flatly.

"You're an actress, aren't you?"

Despite herself, Coco looked up. He'd touched a nerve, "I might be," she replied guardedly.

"*Chorus Line*, right?" Suddenly he was sitting next to her in the booth, and Coco's thin nostrils instinctively pinched together. He smelled like yesterday's dog food, "You're the one who does the smoky number in the red dress?"

Well, who am I to deny it, she thought, and she gave the smallest shrug and a teeny-tiny smile.

"I'm right," grinned the seedy man. "I knew it. Why, you're the best thing in the show. But I guess you get tired of hearing that."

"No," said Coco sincerely.

"You don't belong there, you know." The man leaned toward her confidentially. "If you don't mind my saying so, you're a star. You need a show all to yourself. Anybody can see that, just to look at you. You've got it all. A face. A figure." He moved a little closer.

About two thousand years ago a Greek named Aesop wrote a little book of fables, in which animals revealed all the weaknesses of humankind. And each little fable had a moral. One was called *The Fox and The Crow*. A crow came into possession of a piece of cheese, and the hungry fox wanted it. Knowing this, the crow flew to a high branch, where the fox couldn't follow. Stationing himself below, the fox began praising the crow, calling its feathers beautiful, its beak and form divine. Sing, he begged the crow, just sing for me, so that I may hear your wondrous voice, which I'm certain surpasses that of the nightingale.

Now the crow knew in her heart she couldn't sing for shit, but the fox's words won her over entirely. She opened her mouth to sing. Out fell the cheese, and the fox, snapping it up, ran away, yelling over his shoulder, "You can't sing for shit." The morals: hold on to what you got and don't let anybody sweet-talk you out of it. And: if you're a crow, be a crow. Don't try to wiggle into nightingale's feathers.

The odd thing was, Coco knew all that. If she'd stopped to think, she'd have realized that this creep had picked up on *Show Business*. That's how he'd made her as an actress. And she knew she was strutting around in feathers that didn't belong to her. Her only connection with *A Chorus Line* was waiting on line three times for standing room. And she was pretty street smart. She could put a name to the piece of cheese this grungy fox was probably after. She had tabbed him as a creep the minute she'd laid eyes on him, hadn't she?

But somehow Coco couldn't keep any of that in mind. Wooed by the siren song of admiration, she was busy preening her borrowed feathers.

"I sing, too," she told him, dimpling.

"You do?"

"And play the piano."

"Wow." He grinned at her, revealing dirty, broken teeth, but somehow even that didn't put Coco off. "You see, that's what I mean. You've got it all. But it's more than talent. It's a quality . . . a special quality. You're the kind of person who stands out in a crowd. I was just sitting there having a cup of coffee and a piece of pie and . . . all of a sudden . . . there *you* were. Like some . . . I don't know, some precious jewel in the middle of all this crap. I couldn't take my eyes off you, I really couldn't."

Coco couldn't believe he was speaking the very words she had always dreamed of hearing. Lines she might have written herself, in one of her many fantasies. True, she'd dreamed about hearing them from Bob Fosse's lips, or Michael Bennett's or Tommy Tune's, but a girl can't be too choosy.

"You couldn't take your eyes off me?" she asked softly.

"Honestly. Look, this is probably presumptuous of me. I should probably call your agent . . ."

Now she was hooked. Agent! A flutter of panic grabbed at her throat. "Er . . . I don't . . . relate to agents."

The man in the wrinkled clothes moved even closer. "How do you feel about a screen test?" he breathed.

Whatever doubts Coco might have still nurtured were dispelled by Bruno's angry silence. Now she was more defensive than ever.

"He's a director," she argued, a little too loudly. "A young film director. From the French school. He knows everybody. We sat there and rapped right through the first period. He's real big on me!"

Bruno didn't look up from the keyboard, but he came down harder on the keys to express his hurt feelings.

"I'm impressed," he said coldly.

Coco put her hands on her hips. "You *could* try bein' happy for me," she said.

Bruno shrugged. "You're walking out on us. Why should I be happy?"

"Because this is the kind of chance I've been waiting for," cried Coco. "I knew it was gonna happen, and here it is!"

"Can't it happen later?" asked Bruno. He looked at her for the first time since she'd sprung this on him. His blue eyes were dark with hurt.

The girl shook her head impatiently. "You don't screw around with opportunities, baby. When they come to the door, you better be home."

Bruno smiled sarcastically. "Be home tomorrow. We got a heavy gig tonight."

"I'm sick of bar mitzvahs!" yelled Coco. "And sweet sixteens. And golden anniversaries, and . . ."

"Somebody from Casablanca Records is going to be there," he interrupted quietly.

This took Coco by surprise, and she hesitated for a fraction of a second. Then she thought, someone from Casablanca is *always* gonna be there. Only he never shows up.

"You think I'd walk if it wasn't important?" she demanded.

"I think you might wait one night," said Bruno reasonably.

Coco thought fast. "Look, the guy's leavin' for the Coast," she lied. "He wants my footage in the can to take with him."

"If you cared about us . . ."

"There's plenty of people who sing around here,"

she interrupted. The word "cared" was making her uncomfortable.

"They're not you!" shouted Bruno, exploding suddenly into rage.

Coco took a step backward. She'd never heard him yell like this before. Shy Bruno. Quiet Bruno. Easygoing Bruno.

"Nobody's me. Can I help it? This is my big chance, Bruno. I'm not blowin' it."

Bruno shook his head, marveling at her ironclad cool. "You really don't care, do you?" he asked softly.

Coco shrugged one slim shoulder. "Be reasonable, will you? A screen test doesn't come around every day. You've got to understand that." She put a beseeching hand on his shoulder.

But Bruno shrugged off her hand. He was stunned. Because he could never do a thing like this to her, he'd assumed she could never do it to him. Boy, how wrong can a guy be? What a schmuck he was. "You don't give a damn," he said in a near-whisper. "The band doesn't matter . . . I don't matter . . ."

Coco turned away from him impatiently. "I told you. Get an understudy."

Still lost in his new revelation, Bruno could only stare at her in amazement. For the first time, he seemed to be seeing Coco as she really was—driving, ambitious, possessed by the consuming desire for fame. Above anything else, fame. He was so happy when they'd started going together, happy to be with her, happy to be making her forget Leroy.

Leroy! For the first time it hit him. How easily she'd gone from Leroy to him. How little she must have cared. Leroy was the best dancer in the school,

Bruno the best musician. As simple as that. Coco wanted the best, took only the best. For reasons having nothing to do with him. What a kick in the head!

"I'm an asshole," he said softly.

Coco heaved a very dramatic sigh. "No," she told him flatly. "You just ain't a professional yet."

Funny, she didn't remember him as quite so dirty-looking. Her fantasy had cleaned his fingernails, pressed his clothes and washed his hair. Seeing him again, as if for the first time, brought back all of Coco's first impressions. Creep. Gamely, she fought them down. People of talent were different from the average man. What was the word she was looking for? Ido . . . idiosyncrasies, that was it. The man was entitled to a few of those.

But if he was such a big director, how come he lived in this roach-infested rattrap of a building? A real tenement, one of the rundown single-room-occupancy hotels that infest the Times Square area. Just walking up the stairs of the old building had turned Coco off; the smell of rotting garbage seemed to be coming right out of the walls.

The man's eyes glittered as he let Coco in. The cheap little efficiency apartment was no cleaner than the hallways outside, and smelled nearly as bad. Added to the garbage smell were the odors of unwashed clothing and cheap beer. Coco hesitated in the doorway. There was nobody else in the apartment.

"Am I early?" she asked.

234

"It's okay. Let me take your coat."

She took a step inside and looked around. The room was barely furnished, except for beer cans. But professional floor lights stood on either side of a video camera. The camera was aimed at a red sofa, covered in tattered velvet, that stood in front of a backdrop of non-reflective photographic paper. On a table to the right of the camera setup stood a video monitor, a single blank eye.

Coco shrugged out of her coat. She had dressed very carefully for the screen test, using all the makeup and hairstyle techniques she'd learned at P.A. A check in the mirror before she left home told her she looked dynamite, but now her confidence was beginning to fray just a little around the edges.

"Uh, where's the crew?"

"You're looking at him."

That's what I was afraid of. Out loud, all she said was "Oh."

"I like to be totally in control of the creative product. Like Godard." When he saw that this rang no bell with Coco, he added, "Jean-Luc Godard" in explanation, but Coco still drew a blank.

"You know that guy?" he asked her.

She took a shot. "French?"

"*Oui.* You see his movies?"

"Oh, sure," she lied.

"Then you know what I'm talking about."

"Yeah. Of course." Coco was not about to admit her ignorance, or her feeling of sudden vulnerability.

He was fiddling with the video camera now, looking through the lens to check the focus. "I belong to the *auteur* school of filmmaking," he informed her, mangling the French word atrociously. "More the . . . Mediterranean approach, you know? Can I get you a beer?"

"Uh, no thanks," said Coco nervously. A feeling of uncertainty was beginning to grow inside her, and she was afraid to give it a name. "I'm easy. I just . . . got a lot on my mind."

"Feeling guilty?"

The question, coming out of nowhere, surprised her and she jumped a little. "Don't." He smiled. "The show goes on." His smile was not one to inspire confidence. "Understudies need the exercise," he told her blandly. "You're doing someone a big favor. Sit here, please." He indicated the sofa.

Coco sat down gingerly and watched the man fiddle with the lights. Although the room was slightly cold, she found herself beginning to sweat a little.

"So. You like art films," he said, taking a reading on a light meter.

"Antonioni and those people? Sure. It beats watching 'Laverne and Shirley,' " she cracked, hoping to get her spirits up. This test could be very important to her career, and she didn't want to screw it up.

Now he had the camera focused on her and was looking at her through the lens. "That's wonderful," he said softly. "Your face is wonderful. You have a natural rapport with the camera, did you know that? It's something special. Some performers can make love to the camera. Garbo did, Marilyn did. So could you." His voice was breathless, oily, but Coco heard the words, not the tone. The crow enjoying the blandishments of Mr. Fox.

"Yeah?" She smiled, forgetting the cheese.

"Your blouse. Could you take it off?"

It was like getting doused with a pail of cold water. Coco couldn't believe her ears, and yet part of her must have known all along that this was inevitable.

"What's the matter?" he asked her softly.

"Are you kidding?" Coco found it difficult to get the words out.

"Huh?" The man acted genuinely surprised. "No, I'm not kidding. Really, you're acting like some dumb school kid all of a sudden." He sounded annoyed.

"I'm sorry," said Coco, her eyes filling with tears.

"I thought you were a professional actress!"

"I am!" cried the girl.

"Then what's the problem?" he asked her blandly. He never looked at her directly, but kept his eye glued to the lens of the video camera.

Coco fought down the rising sense of being trapped. This was a screen test. She was a professional. Although all her instincts told her to grab her coat and get her ass out of there, her need to believe kept her pinned to the sofa. This *had* to be a break for her, it had to! The sudden thought of Bruno, playing without her to an executive from Casablanca Records, rose unbidden to her mind. It only made her more determined than ever to succeed with this.

Don't be a fool, said her inner feelings. This guy's a flake, a pervert with a camera, a sick voyeur. Out. Get out. That videotape ain't goin' nowhere 'cept into his personal library of dirty movies. If you move fast you can probaby get to Brooklyn in time to make the bar mitzvah. Kick the "understudy" out and wind up with a recording contract. If you stay here, you're hurting Bruno's chances as well as your own. Get out. Now.

But Coco couldn't afford to listen, couldn't afford to admit to herself that she'd been wrong. Already her hands had moved slowly up to her blouse, and slowly her fingers were working on the buttons, until she had undone them all. Slowly, she slipped the blouse off and sat facing the camera. She wore no bra, and her small breasts were bare.

"That's beautiful," the fox oozed. "Beautiful." He was breathing hard now, his eye pressed to the camera. "Could you put one arm up over the sofa," he ordered. "Yeah, like that. Good. Smile for me. More. Open your mouth a little. That's right. Like Marilyn. Beautiful! Oh, yes . . . Mmmmm. You're special, all right. Wet your lips. Lay back a little. Relax. That's right. That's right. That's beautiful. Oh, yes, you've got it all . . ."

Mechanically, Coco obeyed, facing the camera, shutting out the sight of the sicko and the sound of his rasping voice. She had to believe. She had to keep believing. She couldn't have thrown away a genuine chance for this. It wasn't her karma. No, this had to be the real thing. Had to be. Her chance. Her big chance. Name up in lights. Fortune and fame. Fame. It was gonna happen for her. Soon. Fame. She knew it. She was never wrong.

2

"YOU see Sherwood?" Leroy Johnson demanded of the monitor in the English office.

"She's having time off to be with her husband."

"I didn't know she had a husband."

"I think he's sick," said the monitor, riffling through a set of assignments.

"He'd have to be to be her husband," sneered Leroy.

The monitor shook his head, looking concerned. "No, I think he's quite bad. He's in University Hospital. He's not so old, either. But they say he may die."

Leroy looked at the boy impassively for a moment, then turned suddenly and stalked out of the office.

Barbara Sherwood sat alone on the bench in the hospital corridor. She'd been there so long it seemed to her that she'd been born there. The waiting was tearing her to pieces. Not to know . . .

If they said he was going to get better slowly she would wait there happily for a thousand years. If they said he was going to die . . . well, she'd have to learn to bear it. But this not knowing, those doctors shaking their heads and giving her hope at the same time . . . And seeing Jim lying there, not recognizing her, his eyelids barely fluttering, grotesque tubes sticking out of him everywhere. Her Jim, so active, so vital, so much a man! Now he was hooked up to a life-support system that might not even support his life. And she was left here like a seal on a rock, waiting for something to happen.

She paid no attention to the sound of footsteps coming toward her down the corridor. The doctors and nurses walked so softly in their rubber-heeled shoes, and this couldn't be one of them. It was a clicking stride, and it meant nothing to her. Not even when the footsteps stopped at the bench. It was a moment or two before she looked up.

When she first saw him, she didn't recognize him. The school and everybody in it were light-years away from her now, like something from a different life. And the tears in her eyes made it difficult for her to recognize anybody. The doctors and nurses were nameless and faceless to her. For days now she had been living in a world of anonymous hospital white, and the boy's brown and brooding face intruded slowly into her consciousness.

"Leroy?" she croaked at last.

Leroy Johnson had never seen a white woman cry before. They cried ugly. Their noses got all red, and their eyelids, and their faces puffed out like the belly of a dead fish. I got no time for this, he thought.

"You ever heard of Alvin Ailey?" he demanded brusquely.

Mrs. Sherwood stared at him. "He's a wonderful choreographer," she said uncertainly. What was the boy driving at?

"He wants me to join his company."

Mrs. Sherwood was stunned by Leroy's lack of tact in her painful situation. "Congratulations," she said, half-sarcastically.

"I can't if you flunk me out," Leroy went on doggedly, ignoring her tears.

Mrs. Sherwood shook her head helplessly. "Look, I'm sorry, I really don't think this is the time to . . ."

"I *have* to graduate," he broke in. Under his cool exterior, he was astonished at himself. What was he doing here in this hospital, hassling this woman while her husband was dying? It could wait. He knew it wasn't the time or the place, but somehow his feet had carried him here, and he didn't understand why.

"You should have thought of that four years ago," snapped Mrs. Sherwood.

"Where I come from it don't pay to read and speak white," he told her coldly. But underneath, his feelings were in turmoil.

I can't deal with this, Mrs. Sherwood thought wildly. I really can't. "Not now, Leroy," she pleaded wearily.

But Leroy found it impossible to go. He wanted to say something to this woman, but he didn't know what it was. He couldn't find the words to articulate his need. But the need was there all the same. "Maybe I

241

didn't say it right, but you've been down real hard on me," he told her.

"Whatever you say, Leroy. Go home."

"I stopped going home a long time ago, but you didn't know that, did you?"

Mrs. Sherwood shook her head wearily. "Don't lecture me, Leroy."

Leroy found it impossible to stop. Bitter words poured out of him with an intensity that caught them both by surprise.

"You people make a big deal about pulling us out of the gutter but you still don't want to eat with us. You know where that leaves people like me? *No* where."

"I don't want to hear it," said Mrs. Sherwood angrily. Leave me alone. Let me sit here in peace and wait for my husband to die.

"You're *going* to hear it," insisted the boy, his large hands knotting into fists. "I'm going to be a dancer . . . a good dancer."

"Get out of here, Leroy."

"You know who says so? *Me.* And you with your bitterness and your hang-ups aren't gonna . . ."

"Leave me alone!" It was half a plea, half a demand.

". . . keep me down 'cause I can't read stories I can see on TV every night of the week . . ."

Mrs. Sherwood's loud voice shattered the hospital silence. "Don't you kids ever stop to think of anyone but yourself for a moment?" she screamed. "For God's sake, leave me alone!" And she burst out into bitter weeping.

Leroy watched her for a minute. He realized that

he was responsible for bringing her to this. Oddly, it pleased a part of him, for he knew now that it was partly why he had come—to make contact with her, to elicit an emotion, almost any emotion. Suddenly, he could articulate to himself what he wanted to tell her. You care. You are the only one who cared a damn about anything I ever did. You wanted me to be better. You forced me to be better. You were wrong sometimes, but I was wrong too. You rode me to hell and back, because you saw something in me that nobody else ever saw. But he could not speak the words.

Instead, Leroy sat down at the other end of the bench. Still weeping, Mrs. Sherwood was rummaging in her purse, looking in vain for a handkerchief. She'd used up all her damn tissues, and she was crying so hard, she couldn't see.

"How's your old man?" asked Leroy quietly.

Sherwood shook her head hopelessly. "Shit," she said, and in that simple word was all her fear and despair.

Reaching into his back pocket, Leroy pulled out a clean handkerchief. "Here," he said.

She looked up and saw the handkerchief being held out to her. A white flag of peace. She took it into her hand and put it to her face, mopping at her eyes, blowing her nose. "Thank you," she said.

Leroy smiled. "I got lotsa handkerchiefs," he said lightly.

Their eyes met, and, wondrously, they smiled at each other. He took her hand in his. You were there when I needed you, he seemed to be saying. Now I'm here when you need me.

Barbara Sherwood blew her nose again. Well, what

243

do you know? she thought. I broke through to him and I never realized it. I actually broke through. Suddenly, she knew that, even if, God forbid, she should lose Jim there would be a reason to go on. There was always a reason to go on. Being a damn good teacher was possibly the best reason in the world to keep moving on.

She and Ralph were out of sync, thought Doris sadly. They didn't seem to be on the same wavelength anymore. It wasn't only that they weren't spending much time together. Ralph had changed. The few minutes he did manage to find for her these days were strained, awkward, even unpleasant. Ralph never talked about their living together anymore, although he seemed to take it for granted that she was his girl and wouldn't see anybody else. In fact, she was spending much more time with Montgomery, as in the old days. But even that had changed. Montgomery was busy writing sketches for the Senior Show. He was even going to direct a segment, and Doris was going to assist him. When they worked together, they hardly ever spoke of Ralph.

He had been playing a little club in Queens, to a crowd of beer drinkers who found everything funny. Say the word "shit" and they cracked up for days. Say "fuck" and it brought the house down. Ralph had been tasting the wine of success, and he found it sweet, even if the wineglasses were very small.

But tonight he was back at Catch a Rising Star,

and it wasn't amateur night, either. It was a real gig, and the audience was hot. Listen to them laughing at Ricky Ferry, the comic who went on ahead of him. They were busting their sides. This was a hot club, the hottest. He'd have them eating out of his hand.

But why was he so goddamn tired? He was so tired, man, wasted. He couldn't face an audience feeling this punk. He wouldn't even be able to hold onto the microphone.

"I need something," Ralph said to Montgomery.

"Sleep," Doris put in. He looked awful; his cheeks were so hollow his jaw looked like a razor blade, and there were dark circles around his eyes. He looked twenty-eight, not eighteen.

Ralph shook his head. "Somethin' to keep me flyin'."

Looks like you've already flown, thought Montgomery. Ralph was really strung out, crashing off too much speed. What he needed was a month in the country, but what he was asking for was drugs.

"Like what?" asked Montgomery.

"Like by way of your witch doctor."

Montgomery shook his curly head. "I don't see Dr. Golden anymore," he said seriously. "Anyway, you're taking too much."

"Thank you, Dr. Marcus Welby. Thank you a whole fuckin' lot," snapped Ralph sarcastically.

"I know what I'm talking about," Montgomery insisted.

"Don't work my case," snapped Ralph.

"I'm your friend."

Ralph threw him a paranoid glare. "Some fuckin' friend. What are you after? Fuckin' faggot!"

245

Cut to the quick by the hurtful unfairness of the charge, Montgomery stood up stiffly. "I gotta go to the bathroom," was all he said as he walked away.

That left Doris and Ralph staring at each other. The expression on her face was making him acutely uncomfortable, and he took out a pack of cigarettes and flipped one up with his thumb, lighting it with a silver lighter. Doris had never seen him with a cigarette before. It was one more example of how out of touch with each other they were.

"You got a problem?" said Ralph nastily.

"We don't see you anymore," answered Doris quietly.

"You see me plenty."

"Asleep in class. Or drinking with your new 'friends' after the shows."

Ralph shrugged carelessly. "After the shows is when everything happens. When all the big names come in. When you get to know people. *The* people. That's what counts. That's why I hang out. Look, I hate drinking. I'm doin' this for my future. For *our* future." He tried to smile.

Doris shook her head decisively. "You're doing this for Freddie. Because *he* did it." Some future. Ralph hanging out on the fringes, trying to break in, getting farther and farther off the planet on his Freddie Prinze trip.

"Maybe," he conceded.

"But he died doing it," said Doris earnestly. If only she could make him understand! "He could have been a real actor."

Ralph raised himself a little from his exhausted slump.

"He *was* a real actor."

"He told *jokes*. He was funny and charming and he made people laugh. That's all."

"That's a lot," Ralph protested.

"But it's not enough. Not for you. You're good, Ralph. Really, seriously good."

Serious. There's that word again. Serious. "Jesus Christ!"

"You're full of rage and pain and . . . love," Doris went on, her eyes begging him to listen. "Not just jokes."

"Jesus Christ!" He turned his face away.

But Doris was persistent. "You're an original. The original Ralph Garcia. You don't have to be someone else. Please don't be someone else. Not yet . . ." She broke off, choked by tears.

Ralph couldn't stand to look at her now. "You're bringin' me down," he accused her.

"I'm sorry." Her voice was very small.

"I gotta go out there in a minute and make people laugh," he shouted. "That takes altitude, you know. I need wings. And you're standin' here playin' Miss Flypaper . . ." He was unaware that his voice was carrying into the main room, breaking into Ricky Ferry's monologue, throwing the comic's timing off.

"I said I was sorry."

"Miss Serious Fuckin' Flypaper!" yelled Ralph. "Gimme a break!"

"What's happening to you?" demanded Doris sorrowfully.

Ralph stood up. "Success," he barked. "Hang on or hang up." With that as his exit line, he headed for the main room to take his introduction.

"Ladies and gentlemen, I wanna introduce you to a young man you're going to be hearing a great deal about in the future," said the MC. "In fact, you've heard a lot from him already," he wisecracked, a reference to Ralph's loud argument with Doris. "A fine talent and a close personal friend . . . we have two kids . . . I want a big hand for Ralph Garcy."

Ralph strode onto the stage to a polite if not generous round of applause. The spotlight hit him right in the eyes, and he winced in pain. He felt like ten pounds of shit in a five-pound sack. But the show must go on.

"Thank you, thank you. Like the man said, my name is Ralph Garcy, and I'm a professional asshole. I see a few amateurs in the audience. That's always encouraging."

He paused as always, waiting for his laugh. When it came, it was small and scattered. Ralph scowled, then noticed Montgomery coming out of the men's room, walking over to Doris.

"Oh, a standing ovation." Nobody laughed.

Ralph was starting to sweat a little. If only the fuckin' light didn't hurt his eyes so much, man! His head was beating like a drum, the skin of the forehead stretched tight over the pain. He turned to a young woman at a table down front.

"What's your name?" he asked her.

She stared back at him, refusing to reply.

"Where are you from?" No answer.

He was getting desperate now. "Tough questions, huh? I know. You're shy, right? I know all about shyness. I had a girlfriend once who was so shy . . . she'd hide in a closet when I came over . . ." His eyes sought out Doris. "Right?" he called after her. Without replying, she got up and walked out of the room. Montgomery stayed behind, watching.

What the hell kind of shithole was this? This place was a toilet, and all these people were bums, bums and morons. There was no getting to them. They were ice-cold. You could bleed to death out here, and they wouldn't move an eyelash. Ralph began to riff hard, desperately reaching for a laugh, any laugh.

"Speaking of closets . . . fifteen thousand roaches came out and marched down my block yesterday, demanding better housing." A laugh here and there.

He's dying up there, thought Montgomery as he watched his friend's anguish. He doesn't have it tonight. Make it short, Ralph, he prayed. Don't prolong the agony. It's like a crucifixion.

"I live in the south Bronx, see?" Ralph said, but there was not a flicker of response. Zombies, man, fuckin' zombies out there. *I Walked with a Zombie* and the sequel, *The Zombie Came Back Alone.* They're destroying me. He was sweating profusely now, and the sweat was chilling his body to the bone.

"I . . . er . . . I don't want to alarm you folks, but according to a recent survey . . . *not* laughing at jokes causes cancer."

He'd lost them now, lost them for good. They sat stony-eyed, waiting for him to get off the stage, waiting to laugh at the next guy.

"Uh, bad taste, huh? Well, okay, you win. Screw you all, and your mothers too. *Chinga tu madre, maricón.*" He slammed the mike back on the stand and left the stage to a scattering of boos.

Gasping and retching, Ralph barely made it to the

dressing room in time to throw up into the sink. His stomach was empty; he was bringing up mostly bile. His mind was spinning with the terrible memory of empty faces without laughter, and the sound of booing. They were booing him.

When he raised his head from the sink, he saw Montgomery standing quietly in the doorway of the dressing room.

"What do *you* want?"

"A pizza sounds good," Montgomery said mildly.

"You want to eat?"

Ralph waved his arms angrily. "Gimme a break, will ya!"

"We could split an Angie special. With anchovies, maybe."

"Anchovies!" shrieked Ralph. "Fuck anchovies. I died tonight and you're talkin' about fuckin' pizza!"

Montgomery shook his head and smiled. "I'm talking about *eating* pizza."

Ralph slammed into a chair in front of the dressing table. His face was white and strained, the corners of his mouth pinched. "Oh, that's funny," he said bitterly. "You're a howl. *You* should have been on that stage tonight. The audience hated *me!*"

Montgomery walked over to Ralph and placed his hand on the thin boy's shoulder. "You had a bad night. That happens."

"Not to me, it doesn't," insisted Ralph stubbornly.

"What do you want, insurance? You're in the wrong business. Performers aren't safe. We're the pie-in-the-face people, remember?"

Ralph managed a tiny smile. "Don't lecture me, Sir Laurence."

Montgomery took his hand off Ralph's shoulder. "All anyone ever promised you was seven classes a day and a hot lunch. The rest is up to you. Back in the Middle Ages, they didn't even want to bury us."

"They do now," Ralph wisecracked. A little color was coming back into his cheeks.

Montgomery was stuffing Ralph's stage jacket into a zippered gym bag. "Not if you're good," he said seriously.

Ralph's eyes met Montgomery's in the reflection of the dressing table mirror. "How do you know? How do you know if you're good?" he asked urgently.

Montgomery shook his head just a little. "Maybe you never know. You just hang in there, I guess." Ralph turned and met Montgomery's look straight on. "Friends help," Montgomery said quietly.

Impulsively, Ralph held out his arms and the two boys hugged. For a moment Ralph felt a twinge of fear, but he realized there was nothing sexual in the embrace. They were friends. Nothing to get hung about.

Suddenly, Ralph laughed, a long, loud laugh. "You know something? Wanna know the weirdest thing? Freddie Prinze—once he'd made it real big—realized that it was everything he hated. Johnny Carson show . . . a Caddy El Dorado . . . a pocket full of 'ludes . . . it was no special shit."

Montgomery held his friend at arm's length, looking earnestly into his eyes. "You're not Freddie, Ralph."

Ralph nodded. "I know. You know something else? Even Freddie didn't want to be Freddie." He chuckled.

"No?"

Ralph grinned widely. "He wanted to be Joe Namath."

They both laughed as any two friends will laugh who have driven out at least some of the demons. Then together they went to Angie's for a pizza. With anchovies.

It didn't seem possible. Where do four years go? It seemed only last week that they had come in as green freshmen, and now they were getting their photos taken for the yearbook. Graduation. Whew! Heavy. The cold cru-ell world was waiting for them out there, ready to sink its fangs into their ankles. But a moving target was harder to hit, and these kids intended to be on the move.

Coco and Bruno had broken up, Ralph and Doris hardly spoke to each other any more. But that was okay. You gotta go it alone if you wanna be swift, and each of them had a separate path to follow anyway. But Bruno and Doris and Ralph would always remember their first serious relationship with affection. And Coco—she was moving too fast to look back over her shoulder. Long ago, she had decided that a good memory was excess baggage. It slowed you down.

Graduation always filled Allen Farrell with mixed emotions. He was so proud of his kids and wished them success, but he was sorry to see them leave. This class had filled him with an unusual amount of satisfaction. Four real talents had risen to the top; he predicted they'd go far. Montgomery, having been accepted to Yale Drama School, was on his way to a distinguished career. Farrell was delighted that the boy showed such promise as a director. Following in his mother's footsteps would probably not have proved the right course for him. And Ralph Garcy . . . well, he'd been in some trouble there for a while, but whatever it was appeared to have blown over. And taken some of the hot air out of his sails. Not that there wasn't plenty left. The boy could get to China and back on hot-air power alone. He still had a long way to go, but he was heading in the right direction.

Doris Finsecker, now, she was a real source of pleasure. In four years she had grown from a timorous mouse of a girl into a budding young woman whose every movement suggested a new feeling of self-worth. Even her voice was stronger, better pitched and placed for projection. She moved better. She was turning into a fine actress.

Mrs. Sherwood had given an inch and Leroy had given an inch. She had assigned him Richard Wright's *Black Boy* instead of Chaucer, and Leroy had actually read it. He'd read it with comprehension and appreciation, and had actually written a thousand words on it. Not only that, he'd cajoled his new girl friend into typing it neatly, and Sherwood had nearly fainted when she saw the paper. She gave it a B minus, and Leroy had passed English. Once he was out of her jurisdiction, Sherwood had drawn a deep breath. Now she could admit that maybe she'd been just a little harsh with him, a tiny bit unfair at times. Thank God none of her other classes held anything like Leroy.

She needed all the energy she could muster to help nurse her husband back to health.

The class was scattering . . . soon they'd be out of high school and into the next phases of their lives. Whether they would go on to achieve fame was a matter for the future to decide. Farrell hoped that first they'd gain the maturity they would need to cope with the anguish of rejections that were sure to come. He fervently hoped that they would also find happiness under the bright lights of fame.

Now all that was left was the Senior Day show. They'd worked like dogs to make it the best damn show that anybody had ever seen. Even Bruno's father and Uncle Mario had pitched in. They'd come in after their shifts were over, and rewired the auditorium with heavy-duty cable, so Bruno's amps and the electrified instruments wouldn't blow the lights again. Especially on this night of nights, with parents, teachers, agents, and even casting directors sitting in the auditorium.

Montgomery had worked on the book, and Bruno had turned out a stunning score that was half rock and roll, half classical in its inspiration. It made Shorofsky grind his teeth, but it also set his feet to tapping. This was, after all, nearly the twenty-first century, and he might as well join in just this once.

Montgomery's book was based on his favorite Walt Whitman poem, "I Sing the Body Electric," and it was a joyful celebration of youth and life and faith in the future. Miss Berg had worked on the choreography, but Leroy had choreographed his own part—he was to represent the spirit of Now, and he was damn well gonna blow everybody away with this one! Talk about dancin', keep your eyes on Leroy.

They had been working for months, rehearsing in their separate departments, then holding a series of mass rehearsals that put together the music, words and dancing. When the dress rehearsal was over, the faculty agreed that it was the most impressive Senior Day show ever. United by a stunning chorale and by the power of the amplified music, the actors and dancers had melded into one being—movement and voice, a being that lifted you up from your seat and carried you into their future.

But wait. Now is the time to be quiet. Take your seat. The curtain is going up.

JOHN D. MACDONALD

*"The king of the adventure novel" John D. MacDonald is
one of the world's most popular authors of mystery and
suspense. Here he is at his bestselling best.*

CONDOMINIUM	23525	$2.25
ALL THESE CONDEMNED	14239	$1.50
APRIL EVIL	14128	$1.75
BALLROOM OF THE SKIES	14143	$1.75
THE BEACH GIRLS	14081	$1.75
THE BRASS CUPCAKE	14141	$1.75
A BULLET FOR CINDERELLA	14106	$1.75
CANCEL ALL OUR VOWS	13764	$1.75
CLEMMIE	14015	$1.75
CONTRARY PLEASURE	14104	$1.75
THE CROSSROADS	14033	$1.75
DEADLOW TIDE	14166	$1.75
DEADLY WELCOME	13682	$1.50
DEATH TRAP	13557	$1.50
THE DECEIVERS	14016	$1.75
THE DROWNERS	13582	$1.75
THE EMPTY TRAP	14185	$1.75
THE END OF THE NIGHT	14192	$1.75
THE LAST ONE LEFT	13958	$1.95

This offer expires 1/24/81   8004-2